FRANZ KAFKA
METAMORPHO
& SOME OTHER STORIES.

Terrible idea.*
Please revise.

NO. BECAUSE

HEATHEN EDITIONS
THEIR BOOKS. OUR WAY.

Published in the good ole United States of America
by Heathen Editions, an imprint of
Heathen Creative
P.O. Box 588
Point Pleasant, WV 25550-0588

Heathen Editions are available at quantity discounts.
For information and more tomfoolery, check us out online:

heatheneditions.com

@heatheneditions
#heathenedition

Metamorphosis first published as *Die Verwandlung* 1915
Heathen Edition published June 6, 2023

English Translation by Ian C. Johnston
Book and cover design by Sheridan Cleland
Set in 11pt. Garamond Premier Pro
Titles in Wicked Grit
Handwriting in hardcore pen

ISBN: 978-1-948316-33-0

FIRST HEATHEN EDITION

"One of the few great and perfect works of the poetic imagination written . . . there is nothing which *The Metamorphosis* could be surpassed by."
—Elias Canetti

"Kafka articulates the anguish of being human." —Ernst Pawel

"Without sci-fi trappings of any kind, *The Metamorphosis* forces us to think in terms of analogy, of reflexive interpretation, though it is revealing that none of the characters in the story, including Gregor, ever does think that way."
—David Cronenberg

"The world of Kafka's writing is so bizarre, so alienated, so grotesque that a both humorous and anguished incongruity arises from the juxtaposition of subject and style, absurdity and realism."
—Joachim Neugroschel

"*The Metamorphosis* conveys Kafka's essential vision: to be a writer is to be condemned to irreparable estrangement."
—Stanley Corngold

"You will mark Kafka's style. Its clarity, its precise and formal intonation in such striking contrast to the nightmare matter of his tale. No poetical metaphors ornament his stark black-and-white story. The limpidity of his style stresses the dark richness of his fantasy. Contrast and unity, style and matter, manner and plot are most perfectly integrated."
—Vladimir Nabokov

"Here was a story that defied logic completely and with complete conviction, and it meant something. I wanted to read the story over and over. I have read it countless times since. I'm fascinated by Gregor's loneliness, by his disintegration. And I know I'm reading one of the finest statements ever made on alienation and cruelty, on how we will kill those whom we will not love and will not try to save."
—Anne Rice

OSIS

OSIS

CONTENTS

METAMORPHOSIS
& SOME OTHER STORIES.

HEATHENRY:
THOUGHTS ON THE TEXT.

We've been working on this book to varying degrees for five years, and it has experienced three major reconfigurations before we finally landed on this version you now bear.

At some point we realized that attempting to assign order to these particular short stories was very similar to how one might organize songs on a mixtape. You remember those, right? What we mean is that a good mixtape back in the day had a natural flow to it, one song naturally led into the next song so that the result was a satisfying experience as a whole. Absurdism was Kafka's forte and so we let that be our guide for the story order of this — if you will — Kafka "mixtape."

Little ~~editing~~ Heathening was required on our part as we've only corrected a few stray punctuation errors. We've also appended over 30 footnotes where (we thought) necessary.

Lastly, if you can't tell by the cover, we had a lot of fun with this one! Especially after discovering Kafka's directive for any *Metamorphosis* cover art, which everyone everywhere has seemed to patently ignore for the most part. Naturally, our first thought after discovering that was, "How can we Kafka Kafka? Should we Kafka Kafka? Would Kafka Kafka Kafka? If Kafka Kafkaed Kafka, then how would Kafka Kafka Kafka?" *Et voila!*

Given what lies ahead, it seems masochistic to say, but **enjoy!**

FRANZ KAFKA

METAMORPHO[SIS]

1

One morning, as Gregor Samsa was waking up from anxious dreams, he discovered that in his bed he had been changed into a monstrous verminous bug. He lay on his armor-hard back and saw, as he lifted his head up a little, his brown, arched abdomen divided up into rigid bow-like sections. His blanket perched high on this belly could hardly stay in place; it seemed about to slide off completely. His numerous legs, pitifully thin in comparison to the rest of his circumference, flickered helplessly before his eyes.

"What's happened to me?" he thought. It was no dream. His room, a proper room for a human being, only somewhat too small, lay quietly between the four well-known walls. Above the table, on which an unpacked collection of sample cloth goods was spread out—Samsa was a traveling salesman—hung the picture which he had cut out of an illustrated magazine a little while ago and set in a pretty gilt[1] frame. It was a picture of a woman with a fur hat and a fur boa. She sat erect, lifting up in the direction of the viewer a solid fur muff into which her entire forearm had disappeared.

Gregor's glance then turned to the window. The dreary weather—you could hear the rain drops falling on the metal window ledge—made him quite melancholy.

---

[1] Covered thinly with gold leaf or gold paint.

"Why don't I keep sleeping for a little while longer and forget all this foolishness?" he thought. But this was entirely impractical, for he was used to sleeping on his right side; and in his present state he could not get himself into this position. No matter how hard he threw himself onto his right side, he always rolled onto his back again. He must have tried it a hundred times, closing his eyes so that he would not have to see the wriggling legs, and gave up only when he began to feel a light, dull pain in his side that he had never felt before.

"O God," he thought, "what a demanding job I've chosen! Day in, day out, on the road. The stresses of selling are much greater than the actual work going on at head office, and, in addition to that, I still have to cope with the problems of traveling, the worries about train connections, irregular bad food, temporary and constantly changing human interactions, which never come from the heart. To hell with it all!"

He felt a slight itching on the top of his abdomen. He slowly pushed himself on his back closer to the bed post so that he could lift his head more easily, and found the itchy part, which was entirely covered with small white spots. He did not know what to make of them and wanted to feel the place with a leg, but he retracted it immediately, for the contact felt like a cold shower all over him.

He slid back again into his earlier position.

"This getting up early," he thought, "makes a man quite idiotic. A man must have his sleep. Other traveling salesmen live like harem women. For instance, when I come back to the inn during the course of the morning to write up the necessary orders, these gentlemen are just sitting down to breakfast. If I were to try that with my boss, I'd be fired on the spot. Still, who knows whether that mightn't be really good for me. If it weren't for my parents' sake, I'd have quit ages ago. I would've gone to the boss and told him just what I think from the bottom of my heart. He would've fallen right off his desk! How weird it is for him to sit up at that desk, talking down to the employee from way up there—and even more weird because the boss has trouble hearing, so the employee has to step up quite close to him. Anyway, I haven't completely given up that hope yet. Once I've got together the money to pay off my parents' debt to him—that should take another five or six years—I'll do it for sure. Then I'll make my big break. In any case, right now I have to get up. My train leaves at five o'clock."

He looked over at the alarm clock ticking away on the chest of drawers. "Good God!" he thought. It was half past six, and the hands were going quietly on. It was even past the half hour, already nearly quarter to. Could the alarm have failed to ring? You could see from the bed that it was properly set for four o'clock. Certainly it had rung. Yes, but was it possible to sleep peacefully through that noise which made the furniture shake? Now, it is true he had not slept peacefully, but evidently he had slept all the more deeply. Still, what should he do now? The next train left at seven o'clock. To catch that one, he would have to go in a mad rush. The case of samples was not packed up yet, and he really did not feel particularly bright and lively. And even if he caught the train, there was no avoiding a blowup with the boss; the firm's errand boy would have waited for the five o'clock train and reported the news of his absence long ago. He was the boss's minion, without backbone or intelligence. Well then, what if he reported in sick? But that would be extremely embarrassing and suspicious, because during his five years' service Gregor had not been sick even once. The boss would certainly come with the doctor from the health insurance company and would reproach his parents for their lazy son and cut short all objections by asking for the insurance doctor's comments; for this doctor, everyone was completely healthy but really lazy about work. And besides, would the doctor in this case be totally wrong? Apart from a really excessive drowsiness after the long sleep, Gregor, in fact, felt quite well and even had a really strong appetite.

As he was thinking all this over in the greatest haste, without being able to make the decision to get out of bed—the alarm

pt. ends p. 19

clock was indicating exactly quarter to seven—there was a cautious knock on the door by the head of the bed.

"Gregor," a voice called—it was his mother—"it's quarter to seven. Don't you want to be on your way?"

That soft voice! Gregor was startled when he heard his own voice answering. It was clearly and unmistakably the voice he'd had before, but in it was intermingled, as if from below, an irrepressible, painful squeaking, which left the words positively distinct only in the first moment and distorted them in the reverberation, so that anyone listening did not know if he had heard correctly. Gregor wanted to answer in detail and explain everything, but in these circumstances he confined himself to saying, "Yes, yes, thank you Mother. I'm getting up right away."

Because of the wooden door the change in Gregor's voice was not really noticeable outside, so his mother calmed down with this explanation and shuffled off. However, as a result of the short conversation, the other family members became aware that Gregor was unexpectedly still at home, and already his father was knocking on one side door, weakly but with his fist. "Gregor, Gregor," he called out, "what's going on?" And, after a short while, he urged him on again in a deeper voice: "Gregor! Gregor!"

At the other side door, however, his sister knocked lightly. "Gregor? Are you all right? Do you need anything?"

Gregor directed answers in both directions: "I'll be ready right away." He made an effort with the most careful articulation and inserted long pauses between the individual words to remove everything remarkable from his voice. His father turned back to his breakfast. However, his sister whispered, "Gregor, open the door—I beg you." Gregor had no intention of opening the door; he congratulated himself on his precaution, acquired from traveling, of locking all doors during the night, even at home.

First he wanted to stand up quietly and undisturbed, get dressed, above all have breakfast, and only then consider further action, for—he noticed this clearly—by thinking things over in bed he would not reach a reasonable conclusion. He remembered that before now in bed he had often felt some light pain or other, which was perhaps the result of an awkward lying position, and which later, once he stood up, turned out to be purely imaginary, and he was eager to see how his present fantasies would gradually dissipate. That the change in his voice was nothing other than the onset of a cold, an occupational illness of commercial travelers, of that he had not the slightest doubt.

It was very easy to throw aside the blanket. He needed only to push his stomach out a little, and it fell by itself. But to continue was difficult, particularly because he was so unusually wide. He needed arms and hands to push himself upright. Instead of these, however, he had only many small limbs, which were incessantly moving with very different motions and which, in addition, he was unable to control. If he wanted to bend one of them, then it was the first to extend itself, and if he finally succeeded doing what he wanted with this limb, in the meantime all the others, as if left free, moved around in an excessively painful agitation. "But I must not stay in bed uselessly," said Gregor to himself.

At first he wanted to get out of bed with the lower part of his body, but this lower part—which, by the way, he had not yet looked at and which he also could not picture clearly—proved itself too difficult to move. The attempt went so slowly. When, having become almost frantic, he finally hurled himself forward with all his force and without thinking, he chose his direction incorrectly, and he hit the lower bedpost hard. The violent pain he felt revealed to him that the lower part of his body was at the moment probably the most sensitive.

Thus, he tried to get his upper body out of the bed first and turned his head carefully toward the edge of the bed. He managed to do this easily, and in spite of its width and weight his body mass at last slowly followed the turning of his head. But as he finally extended his head beyond the bed into the air, he became anxious about moving forward any further in this manner, for if he allowed himself eventually to fall by this process, it would really take a miracle to prevent his head from getting injured. And at all costs he must not lose consciousness right now. He preferred to remain in bed.

But after a similar effort it was no different. He lay there again, sighing as before, and once again saw his small limbs fighting one another, if anything even worse than earlier, and did not see any chance of imposing quiet and order on this arbitrary movement. He told himself again that he could not possibly remain in bed and that it might be the most reasonable thing to sacrifice everything if there was even the slightest hope of getting himself out of bed in the process. At the same time, however, he did not forget to keep reminding himself periodically of the fact that calm—indeed the calmest—reflection might be much better than confused decisions. At such moments, he directed his gaze as precisely as he could toward the window, but unfortunately a glance at the morning mist, which concealed even the other side of the narrow street, offered little to make him more confident or cheerful. "It's already seven o'clock," he told himself at the latest sounds from the alarm clock, "already seven o'clock and still such a fog." And for a little while longer he lay quietly with weak breathing, as if perhaps waiting for normal and natural conditions to re-emerge out of the complete stillness.

But then he said to himself, "Before it strikes a quarter past seven, whatever happens I must be completely out of bed. Besides, by then someone from the office will arrive to inquire about me, because the office will open before seven o'clock." And he made an effort then to rock his entire body length out of the bed with a uniform motion. If he let himself fall out of the bed in this way, his head, which in the course of the fall he intended to lift up sharply, would probably remain uninjured. His back seemed to be hard; nothing would really happen to that as a result of the fall onto the carpet. His greatest reservation was a worry about the loud noise which the fall must create and which presumably would arouse, if not fright, then at least concern on the other side of all the doors. Nevertheless, he had to take that chance.

As Gregor was already in the process of lifting himself half out of bed—the new method was more of a game than an effort; he needed only to rock with a series of jerks—it struck him how easy all this would be if someone were to come to his aid. Two strong people—he thought of his father and the servant girl—would have been quite sufficient. They would only have had to push their arms under his arched back to get him out of the bed, to bend down with their load, and then merely to exercise patience so that he could complete the flip onto the floor, where his diminutive legs would then, he hoped, acquire a purpose. Now, quite apart from the fact that the doors were locked, should he really call out for help? In spite of all his distress, he was unable to suppress a smile at this idea.

He had already got to the point where, by rocking more strongly, he was making it very difficult for himself to keep his balance, and very soon he would finally have to make a final decision, for in five minutes it would be a quarter past seven. Then there was a ring at the door of the apartment. "That's someone from the office," he told himself, and he almost froze, while his small limbs only danced around all the faster. For one moment everything remained still. "They aren't opening the door," Gregor said to himself, caught up in some absurd hope. But of course then, as usual, the servant girl with her firm tread went to the door and opened it. Gregor needed to hear only the first word of the visitor's greeting to recognize immediately who it was, the manager himself. Why was Gregor the only one condemned to work in a firm where the slightest lapse would attract the greatest suspicion? Were all the employees collectively, one and all, scoundrels? Among them was there then no truly devoted person who, if he failed to use just a couple of hours in the morning for office work, would become abnormal from pangs of conscience and really be in no state to get out of bed? Would it not have been enough to let an apprentice make inquiries, if such questioning was even necessary? Must the manager himself come, and in the process must it be demonstrated to the entire innocent family that the investigation of this suspicious circumstance could be

pt. ends p. 19

entrusted only to the intelligence of the manager? More as a consequence of the excited state in which this idea put Gregor than as a result of any actual decision, he swung himself with all his might out of the bed. There was a loud thud, but not a real crash. The fall was absorbed somewhat by the carpet and, in addition, his back was more elastic than Gregor had thought. For that reason the dull noise was not quite so conspicuous. But he had not held his head up with sufficient care and had bumped it. He turned his head, irritated and in pain, and rubbed it on the carpet.

"Something has fallen in there," said the manager in the next room on the left. Gregor tried to imagine to himself whether anything similar to what was happening to him today could have also happened at some point to the manager. At least one had to concede the possibility of such a thing. However, as if to give a rough answer to this question, the manager now, with a squeak of his polished boots, took a few determined steps in the next room.

From the neighboring room on the right the sister was whispering to inform Gregor: "Gregor, the manager is here."

"I know," said Gregor to himself. But he did not dare make his voice loud enough so that his sister could hear.

"Gregor," his father now said from the neighboring room on the left, "Mr. Manager has come and is asking why you did not leave on the early train. We don't know what we should tell him. Besides, he also wants to speak to you personally. So please open the door. He will be good enough to forgive the mess in your room."

In the middle of all this, the manager called out in a friendly way, "Good morning, Mr. Samsa."

"He is not well," said his mother to the manager, while his father was still talking at the door, "He is not well, believe me, Mr. Manager. Otherwise how would Gregor miss a train? The young man has nothing in his head except business. I'm almost angry that he never goes out in the evening. Right now he's been in the city eight days, but he's been at home every evening. He sits here with us at the table and reads the newspaper quietly or studies his travel schedules. Working with wood can be quite a diversion for him; he busies himself with fretwork. For instance, he cut out a small frame over the course of two or three evenings. You'd be amazed how pretty it is. It's hanging right inside the room. You'll see it immediately, as soon as Gregor opens the door. Anyway, I'm happy that you're here, Mr. Manager. By ourselves, we would never have made Gregor open the door. He's so stubborn, and he's certainly not well, although he denied that this morning."

"I'm coming right away," said Gregor slowly and deliberately, without moving, so as not to lose one word of the conversation.

"My dear lady, I cannot explain it to myself in any other way," said the manager; "I hope it is nothing serious. On the other hand, I must also say that we business people, luckily or unluckily, however one looks at it, very often simply have to overcome a slight indisposition for business reasons."

"So can Mr. Manager come in to see you now?" asked his father impatiently and knocked once again on the door.

"No," said Gregor. In the neighboring room on the left an awkward stillness descended. In the neighboring room on the right the sister began to sob.

Why did his sister not go to the others? She had probably just got up out of bed now and had not even started to get dressed yet. Then why was she crying? Because he was not getting up and letting the manager in, because he was in danger of losing his position, and because then his boss would badger his parents once again with the old demands? Those were probably unnecessary worries right now. Gregor was still here and was not thinking at all about abandoning his family. At the moment he was lying right there on the carpet, and no one who knew about his condition would have seriously demanded that he let the manager in. In any case, Gregor would not be casually dismissed right away because of this small discourtesy, for which he would find an easy and suitable excuse later on. It seemed to Gregor that it would be far more reasonable to leave him in

pt. ends p. 19

peace at the moment, instead of disturbing him with crying and exhortations. But the others were distressed by their uncertainty, which excused their behavior.

"Mr. Samsa!" The manager was now shouting, his voice raised. "What's the matter? You are barricading yourself there in your room, answering with only a yes and a no, you are making serious and unnecessary trouble for your parents, and you are neglecting—I mention this only incidentally—your commercial duties in a truly unheard-of manner. I am speaking here in the name of your parents and your employer, and I am requesting you in all seriousness to give an immediate and clear explanation. I am amazed. I am amazed. I thought I knew you as a calm, reasonable person, and now you appear suddenly to want to start parading around in strange moods. The Chief indicated to me earlier this very day a possible explanation for your neglect—it concerned the collection of cash entrusted to you a short while ago—but in truth I almost gave him my word of honor that this explanation could not be correct. However, now I see here your unimaginable pigheadedness, and I am totally losing any desire to speak up for you in the slightest. And your position is not at all the most secure. Originally I intended to mention all this to you privately, but since you are letting me waste my time here uselessly, I don't know why the matter shouldn't come to the attention of your parents as well. Your productivity has been very unsatisfactory recently. Of course, it's not the time of year to produce exceptional sales, we recognize that, but a time of year for producing no sales, there is no such thing at all, Mr. Samsa, and such a thing must not be permitted."

"But Mr. Manager," called Gregor, beside himself and, in his agitation, forgetting everything else, "I'm opening the door immediately, this very moment. A slight indisposition, a dizzy spell, has prevented me from getting up. I'm still lying in bed right now. But I'm quite refreshed once again. I'm in the midst of getting out of bed. Just have patience for a short moment! Things are not yet going as well as I thought. But things are all right with me. How suddenly this can overcome someone! Only yesterday evening everything was fine with me. My parents certainly know that. Actually just yesterday evening I had a small premonition. People must have seen that in me. Why did I not report that to the office? But people always think that they'll get over sickness without having to stay at home. Mr. Manager! Take it easy on my parents! There is really no basis for the criticisms which you're now making against me. Nobody has said a word to me about any of this. Perhaps you have not seen the latest orders I sent in. Besides, I'm setting out on a new sales trip on the eight o'clock train; the few hours' rest have made me stronger. Mr. Manager, there's no need for you to wait here any longer. I will be at the office in person right away. Please have the goodness to report that and to convey my respects to the Chief."

While Gregor was quickly blurting all this out, hardly aware of what he was saying, he had moved close to the chest of drawers without effort, probably as a result of the practice he had already had in bed, and now he was trying to raise himself up on it. Actually, he wanted to open the door. He really wanted to let himself be seen and to speak with the manager. He was keen to see what the others who had been asking about him just now would say when they saw him. If they were startled, then Gregor would no longer be burdened by responsibility and could be calm. But if they accepted everything quietly, then he would have no reason to get excited; if he got a move on, he could really be at the station around eight o'clock.

At first he slid down a few times on the smooth chest of drawers. But at last he gave himself a final swing and stood upright there. He was no longer at all aware of the pains in his lower body, no matter how they might still sting. Now he let himself fall against the back of a nearby chair, on the edge of which he braced himself with his small limbs. By doing this he gained control over himself and kept quiet, for he could now hear the manager.

"Did you understand even a single word?" the manager asked the parents, "Is he playing the fool with us?"

pt. ends p. 19

"For God's sake," cried the mother, already in tears, "perhaps he's very ill, and we're upsetting him. Grete! Grete!" she yelled.

"Mother?" called the sister from the other side. They were making themselves understood through Gregor's room. "You must go to the doctor right away. Gregor is sick. Hurry to the doctor. Did you hear Gregor speak just now?"

"That was an animal's voice," said the manager, remarkably quiet in comparison to the mother's cries.

"Anna! Anna!" yelled the father through the hall into the kitchen, clapping his hands, "Fetch a locksmith right away!" The two young women were already running through the hall with swishing skirts—how had his sister dressed herself so quickly?—and pulling open the doors of the apartment. You couldn't hear the doors closing at all. They probably had left them open, as is customary in an apartment where a great misfortune has taken place.

However, Gregor had become much calmer. All right, people did not understand his words anymore, although they seemed clear enough to him, clearer than previously, perhaps because his ears had gotten used to them. But at least people now thought that things were not completely all right with him and were prepared to help him. The confidence and assurance with which the first arrangements had been carried out made him feel good. He felt himself included once again in the circle of humanity and was expecting from both the doctor and the locksmith, without differentiating between them with any real precision, splendid and surprising results. In order to make his voice as clear as possible for the critical conversation which was imminent, he coughed a little. He certainly took care to do this in a really subdued way, since it was possible that even this noise would sound like something different from a human clearing of the throat. He no longer trusted his judgment. Meanwhile in the next room it had become very quiet. Perhaps his parents were sitting with the manager at the table whispering; perhaps they were all leaning against the door and listening.

Gregor pushed himself slowly toward the door, with the help of the easy chair. Then he let go of the chair, threw himself against the door, held himself upright against it—the balls of his tiny limbs had a little sticky stuff on them—and rested there momentarily from his exertion. Next he made an effort to turn the key in the lock with his mouth. Unfortunately it seemed that he had no real teeth. How then was he to grab hold of the key? But to make up for that his jaws were naturally very strong; with their help he managed to get the key actually moving. He did not notice that he was obviously inflicting some damage on himself; a brown fluid was coming out of his mouth, flowing over the key, and dripping onto the floor.

"Just listen," said the manager in the next room. "He's turning the key." For Gregor that was a great encouragement. But they should all have called out to him, including his father and mother, "Come on, Gregor," they should have shouted, "keep going, keep working on the lock!" Imagining that all his efforts were being followed with suspense, he bit down on the key unthinkingly with all the force he could muster. As the key turned more, he danced around the lock. Now he was holding himself upright only with his mouth, and he had to alternate as necessary between hanging onto the key and pressing it down again with the whole weight of his body. The quite distinct click of the lock as it finally snapped open really woke Gregor up. Breathing heavily he said to himself, "So I didn't need the locksmith," and he set his head against the door handle to open the door completely.

Because he'd had to open the door in this way, it swung open really wide without him yet being visible. He first had to edge himself slowly around the door frame, very carefully, of course, if he did not want to fall awkwardly on his back right at the entrance into the room. He was still preoccupied with this difficult movement and had no time to pay attention to anything else, when he heard the manager exclaim a loud "Oh!"—it sounded like the wind whistling—and now he saw him, nearest to the door, pressing his hand against his open mouth and moving

pt. ends p. 19

slowly back, as if an invisible constant force were pushing him away. His mother—in spite of the presence of the manager she was standing here with her hair sticking up on end, still a mess from the night—first looked at his father with her hands clasped, then went two steps toward Gregor and collapsed right in the middle of her skirts, which were spread out all around her, her face sunk on her breast, completely concealed. His father clenched his fist with a hostile expression, as if he wished to push Gregor back into his room, then looked uncertainly around the living room, covered his eyes with his hands, and cried so that his mighty breast shook.

At this point Gregor had still not taken one step into the room; he was leaning his body from the inside against the firmly bolted wing of the door, so that only half his body was visible, as well as his head, tilted sideways, with which he peeped over at the others. Meanwhile it had become much brighter. Standing out clearly from the other side of the street was a section of the end-less gray-black house situated opposite—it was a hospital—with its severe[2] regular windows breaking up the facade. The rain was still coming down, but only in large individual drops visibly and firmly thrown down one by one onto the ground. Countless breakfast dishes were standing piled around on the table, because for his father breakfast was the most important meal time in the day, one which he prolonged for hours by reading various news-papers. Directly across on the opposite wall hung a photograph of Gregor from the time of his military service; it was a picture of him as a lieutenant; smiling and worry free, with his hand on his sword, he demanded respect for his bearing and uniform. The door to the hall was ajar, and since the door to the apartment was also open, you could see out into the landing of the apartment and the start of the staircase going down.

"Now," said Gregor, well aware that he was the only one who had kept his composure, "I'll get dressed right away, pack up the

---

[2] Very plain in style or appearance.

collection of samples, and set off. You'll allow me to set out on my way, will you not? You see, Mr. Manager, I am not pigheaded, and I am happy to work. Traveling is exhausting, but I couldn't live without it. Where are you going, Mr. Manager? To the office? Really? Will you report everything truthfully? A person can be incapable of work momentarily, but that's precisely the best time to remember the earlier achievements and to consider that later, after the obstacles have been removed, the person will certainly work all the more diligently and intensely. I am really so indebted to Mr. Chief—you know that perfectly well. On the other hand, I am concerned about my parents and my sister. I'm in a fix, but I'll work myself out of it again. Don't make things more difficult for me than they already are. Speak up on my behalf in the office! People don't like traveling salesmen. I know that. People think they earn pots of money and thus lead a fine life. People never have any special reason to think through this judgment more clearly. But you, Mr. Manager, you have a better perspective on what's involved than other people—even, I tell you in total confidence, a better perspective than Mr. Chief himself, who in his capacity as the employer may easily shade his decisions at the expense of an employee. You also know well enough that the traveling salesman who is outside the office almost the entire year can become so easily a victim of gossip, coincidences, and groundless complaints, against which it's totally impossible for him to defend himself. For the most part he doesn't hear about them at all, and if he does it's only when he's at home and exhausted after finishing a trip. Then he gets to feel in his own body the nasty consequences, which can't be thoroughly traced back to their origins. Mr. Manager, don't leave without speaking a word indicating to me that you'll at least concede that I'm a little in the right!"

But at Gregor's first words the manager had already turned away, and now he looked back with pursed lips at Gregor over his twitching shoulders. During Gregor's speech he had not been still for a moment but had kept moving away toward the door, without taking his eyes off Gregor, but really gradually, as if there were a secret ban on leaving the room. He was already in the hall, and given the sudden movement with which he finally pulled his foot out of the living room, you could have believed that he had just burned his sole. In the hall, however, he stretched his right hand out away from his body toward the staircase, as if some almost supernatural relief was waiting for him there.

Gregor realized that he must not under any circumstances allow the manager to go away in this frame of mind, if his position in the firm was not to be placed in the greatest danger. His parents did not understand all this very well. Over the long years, they had developed the conviction that Gregor was set up for life in this firm and, in addition, they had so much to do nowadays with their present troubles that all foresight was foreign to them. But Gregor had this foresight. The manager must be detained, calmed down, convinced, and finally won over. The future of Gregor and his family really depended on it! If only his sister had been there! She was clever. She had already cried while Gregor was still lying quietly on his back. And the manager, always a friend of the ladies, would certainly let himself be guided by her. She would have closed the door to the apartment and talked him out of his fright in the hall. But his sister was not even there. Gregor had to deal with it himself.

Without thinking that as yet he did not know anything about his present ability to move, and without thinking that his speech possibly—indeed probably—had once again not been understood, he left the wing of the door, pushed himself through the opening, and tried to go over to the manager, who was already holding the handrail on the landing tight, gripping with both hands in a ridiculous way. But as Gregor looked for something to steady himself, with a small scream he immediately fell down onto his numerous little legs. Scarcely had this happened, when he felt for the first time that morning a general physical well-being. The small limbs had firm floor under them; they obeyed perfectly, as he noticed to his joy, and even strove to carry him forward in the direction he wanted. Right away he believed that the final amelioration [3] of all his suffering was immediately at hand. But at the very moment when he lay on the floor rocking in a restrained manner quite close to and directly across from his mother, who seemed to have totally sunk into herself, she suddenly sprang right up with her arms spread far apart and her fingers extended and cried out, "Help, for God's sake, help!" She held her head bowed down, as if she wanted to view Gregor better, but then she ran senselessly back, contradicting that gesture, forgetting that behind her stood the table with all the dishes on it. When she reached the table, she sat down heavily on it, as if absentmindedly, and did not appear to notice at all that next to her coffee was pouring out onto the carpet in a full stream from the large, overturned pot.

"Mother, mother," said Gregor quietly and looked over toward her. The manager had momentarily vanished completely from his mind. On the other hand, when he saw the flowing coffee Gregor could not stop himself snapping his jaws in the air a few times. At that his mother screamed all over again, hurried from the table, and collapsed into the arms of his father, who was rushing toward her. But Gregor had no time right now for his parents—the manager was already on the staircase. With his chin on the banister, the manager looked back for the last time. Gregor made a running start to catch up to him if possible. But the manager must have suspected something, because he made a leap down over a few stairs and disappeared, still shouting "Aah!" The sound echoed throughout the entire stairwell.

Unfortunately, this flight of the manager seemed to bewilder his father completely. Earlier he had been relatively calm. Now instead of running after the manager himself, or at least not hindering Gregor from his pursuit, with his right hand he grabbed hold of the cane that the manager had left behind on a chair with his hat and overcoat. With his left hand, the father grabbed a

---

[3] The act of making something better; improvement.

large newspaper from the table and, stamping his feet on the floor, he set out to drive Gregor back into his room by waving the cane and the newspaper. No request of Gregor's was of any use; no request would even be understood. No matter how willing he was to turn his head respectfully, his father just stomped all the harder with his feet.

Across the room from him his mother had pulled open a window, in spite of the cool weather, and leaning out with her hands on her cheeks, she pushed her face far outside the window. Between the lane and the stairwell a strong draft came up, the curtains on the window flew around, the newspapers on the table rustled, and individual sheets fluttered down over the floor. His father relentlessly pushed his way forward, hissing like a wild man. Now, Gregor still had no practice at all in going backward—it was really very slow going. If Gregor only had been allowed to turn himself around, he would have been in his room right away, but he was afraid to make his father impatient by the time-consuming process of turning around, and each moment he faced the threat of a mortal blow on his back or his head from the cane in his father's hand. Finally Gregor had no other option, for he noticed with horror that he did not understand yet how to maintain his direction going backward. And so he began, amid constantly anxious sideways glances in his father's direction, to turn himself around as quickly as possible, although in truth he could only do this very slowly. Perhaps his father noticed his good intentions, for he did not disrupt Gregor in this motion, but with the tip of the cane from a distance he even directed Gregor's rotating movement now and then.

If only his father had not hissed so unbearably! Because of that Gregor totally lost his head. He was already almost totally turned around, when, always with this hissing in his ear, he just made a mistake and turned himself back a little. But when he finally was successful in getting his head in front of the door opening, it became clear that his body was too wide to go through any further. Naturally his father, in his present mental state, had no idea of, say, opening the other wing of the door a bit to create a suitable passage for Gregor to get through. His single fixed thought was that Gregor must get into his room as quickly as possible. He would never have allowed the elaborate preparations Gregor required to raise himself up and perhaps in this way get through the door. Perhaps with his excessive noise he was now driving Gregor forward as if there were no obstacle. Behind Gregor the sound at this point was no longer like the voice of only a single father. Now it was really no longer a joke, and Gregor forced himself, come what might, into the doorway. One side of his body lifted up. He lay at an angle in the door opening. His one flank was all raw from the scraping. On the white door ugly blotches were left. Soon he was stuck fast and would not have been able to move anymore on his own. The tiny legs on one side hung twitching in the air above, and the ones on the other side were pushed painfully into the floor. Then his father gave him one really strong liberating push from behind, and he scurried, bleeding severely, far into his room. The door was slammed shut with the cane, and then finally it was quiet.

II

Gregor first woke up from his heavy swoon-like [1] sleep in the evening twilight. He would certainly have woken up soon afterward even without any disturbance, for he felt himself sufficiently rested and wide awake; but it appeared to him as if a hurried step and a cautious closing of the door to the hall might have roused him. Light from the electric streetlights lay pale here and there on the ceiling of his room and on the higher parts of the furniture, but down around Gregor it was dark. He pushed himself slowly toward the door, still groping awkwardly with his feelers, which he now learned to value for the first time, to check what was happening. His left side seemed one single long unpleasantly stretched scar, and he really had to hobble on his two rows of legs. In addition, one small leg had been seriously wounded in the course of the morning incident—it was almost a miracle that only one had been hurt—and dragged lifelessly behind.

By the door he first noticed what had really lured him there: it was the smell of something to eat. A bowl stood there, filled with sweetened milk, in which swam tiny pieces of white bread. He almost laughed with joy, for he had an even greater hunger than in the morning, and he immediately dipped his head almost over his eyes down into the milk. But he soon drew it back again

---

[1] As though it happened suddenly and got the better of him.

in disappointment, not just because it was difficult for him to eat on account of his delicate left side—he could eat only if his entire panting body worked in a coordinated way—but also because the milk, which had always been his favorite drink and which his sister had certainly placed there for that reason, did not appeal to him at all. He turned away from the bowl almost with aversion and crept back into the middle of the room.

In the living room, as Gregor saw through the crack in the door, the gas was lit, but where, on other occasions at this time of day, his father was accustomed to read the afternoon newspaper in a loud voice to his mother and sometimes also to his sister, at the moment no sound was audible. Perhaps this reading aloud, about which his sister had always spoken and written to him, had recently fallen out of their general routine. But it was so still all around, in spite of the fact that the apartment was certainly not empty.

"What a quiet life the family leads," said Gregor to himself, and, as he stared fixedly out in front of him into the darkness, he felt a great pride that he had been able to provide such a life for his parents and his sister in such a beautiful apartment. But how would things go if now all tranquility, all prosperity, all contentment should come to a horrible end? In order not to lose himself in such thoughts, Gregor preferred to set himself moving, so he crawled up and down in his room.

Once during the long evening one side door and then the other door were opened just a tiny crack and quickly closed again. Someone presumably had felt they needed to come in but had then thought better of it. Gregor immediately took up a position by the living room door, determined to bring in the hesitant visitor somehow or other, or at least to find out who it might be. But now the door was not opened anymore; Gregor waited in vain. Earlier, when the door had been barred, they had all wanted to come in to him; now, when he had opened one door and when the others had obviously been opened during the day, no one came anymore, and now the keys were stuck in the locks on the outside.

The light in the living room was turned off only late at night, and it was now easy to establish that his parents and his sister had stayed awake all this time, for one could hear them clearly as all three moved away on tiptoe. Now it was certain that no one would come in to Gregor anymore until the morning. Thus, he had a long time to think undisturbed about how he should reorganize his life from scratch. But the high, open room, in which he was compelled to lie flat on the floor, made him anxious, without his being able to figure out the reason, for he had lived in the room for five years. With a half-unconscious turn and not without a little shame he scurried under the couch, where, in spite of the fact that his back was a little cramped and he could no longer lift up his head, he felt very comfortable right away and was sorry only that his body was too wide to fit completely under the couch.

There he remained the entire night, which he spent partly in a state of semi-sleep, out of which his hunger constantly woke him with a start, but partly in a state of worry and murky hopes, which all led to the conclusion that for the time being he would have to keep calm and with patience and the greatest consideration for his family tolerate the troubles which in his present condition he was now forced to cause them.

Already early in the morning—it was still almost night—Gregor had an opportunity to test the power of the decisions he had just made, for his sister, almost fully dressed, opened the door from the hall into his room and looked eagerly inside. She did not find him immediately, but when she noticed him under the couch—God, he had to be somewhere or other, for he could hardly fly away—she got such a shock that, without being able to control herself, she slammed the door shut once again from the outside. However, as if she was sorry for her behavior, she immediately opened the door again and walked in on her tiptoes, as if she was in the presence of a serious invalid or a total

pt. ends p. 41

stranger. Gregor had pushed his head forward just to the edge of the couch and was observing her. Would she really notice that he had left the milk standing, not indeed from any lack of hunger, and would she bring in something else to eat more suitable for him? If she did not do it on her own, he would sooner starve to death than call her attention to the fact, although he had a really powerful urge to dash out from under the couch, throw himself at his sister's feet, and beg her for something or other good to eat. But his sister noticed right away with astonishment that the bowl was still full, with only a little milk spilled around it. She picked it up immediately, not with her bare hands but with a rag, and took it out of the room. Gregor was extremely curious what she would bring as a substitute, and he pictured to himself very different ideas about it. But he never could have guessed what his sister, out of the goodness of her heart, in fact, did. To test his taste, she brought him an entire selection, all spread out on an old newspaper. There were old half-rotten vegetables, bones from the evening meal, covered with a white sauce which had almost solidified, some raisins and almonds, cheese which Gregor had declared inedible two days earlier, a slice of dry bread, a slice with butter, and a slice of salted bread smeared with butter. In addition to all this, she put down the bowl—probably designated once and for all as Gregor's—into which she had poured some water. And out of her delicacy of feeling, since she knew that Gregor would not eat in front of her, she went away very quickly and even turned the key in the lock, so that Gregor could now know that he might make himself as comfortable as he wished. Gregor's small limbs buzzed now that the time for eating had come. His wounds must, in any case, have already healed completely. He felt no handicap on that score. He was astonished at that, and thought about how more than a month ago he had cut his finger very slightly with a knife—and this wound had still hurt the day before yesterday. "Am I now going to be less sensitive?" he thought, already sucking greedily on the cheese, which had strongly attracted him right away, more than all the other foods. Quickly and with his eyes watering with satisfaction, he ate one after the other the cheese, the vegetables, and the sauce. The fresh food, by contrast, did not taste good to him. He could not even bear the smell and carried the things he wanted to eat a little distance away. By the time his sister slowly turned the key as a sign that he should withdraw, he was long finished with everything and now lay lazily in the same spot. The noise immediately startled him, in spite of the fact that he was already almost asleep, and he scurried back again under the couch. But it cost him great self-control to remain under the couch, even for the short time his sister was in the room, because his body had filled out somewhat on account of the rich meal and in the narrow space there he could scarcely breathe. In the midst of minor attacks of asphyxiation, he looked at her with somewhat protruding eyes, as his unsuspecting sister swept up with a broom, not just the remnants, but even the foods which Gregor had not touched at all, as if these were also now useless, and as she dumped everything quickly into a bucket, which she closed with a wooden lid, and then carried all of it out of the room. She had hardly turned around before Gregor had already dragged himself out from under the couch, stretched out, and let his body expand.

In this way Gregor now got his food every day, once in the morning, when his parents and the servant girl were still asleep, and a second time after the common noon meal, for his parents were asleep then for a little while, and the servant girl was sent off by his sister on some errand or other. They certainly would not have wanted Gregor to starve to death, but perhaps they could not have endured finding out what he ate (other than by hearsay). Perhaps his sister also wanted to spare them what was possibly only a small grief, for they were really suffering quite enough already.

What sorts of excuses people had used on that first morning to get the doctor and the locksmith out of the house again Gregor was completely unable to ascertain. Since they could not

pt. ends p. 41

understand him, no one, not even his sister, had imagined that he might be able to understand others, and thus, when his sister was in his room, he had to be content with listening now and then to her sighs and invocations to the saints. Only later, when she had grown somewhat accustomed to everything—naturally there could never be any talk of her growing completely accustomed to it—Gregor sometimes caught a comment which was intended to be friendly or could be interpreted as such. "Well, today it tasted good to him," she said, if Gregor had really cleaned up what he had to eat; whereas, in the reverse situation, which gradually repeated itself more and more frequently, she used to say almost sadly, "Now everything has been left again."

But while Gregor could get no new information directly, he did hear a good deal from the room next door, and as soon as he heard voices, he scurried over right away to whichever door it was and pressed his entire body against it. In the early days especially, there was no conversation which was not concerned with him in some way or other, even if only surreptitiously.[2] For two days at all meal times discussions could be heard of how they should now conduct themselves. They also talked about the same subject in the times between meals, for there were always at least two family members at home, since no one really wanted to remain in the house alone and people could not under any circumstances leave the apartment completely empty. In addition, on the very first day the servant girl—it was not completely clear what and how much she knew about what had happened—on her knees had begged his mother to let her go immediately. When she said goodbye about fifteen minutes later, she thanked them for the dismissal with tears in her eyes, as if she was receiving the greatest favor which people had ever shown her there, and, without anyone demanding it from her, she swore a fearful oath not to reveal anything to anyone, not even the slightest detail.

Now his sister had to team up with his mother to do the

---

[2] Secretively.

cooking, although that did not create much trouble because people were eating almost nothing. Again and again Gregor listened as one of them vainly invited another one to eat and received no answer other than, "Thank you. I've had enough," or something like that. And perhaps they had stopped having anything to drink, too. His sister often asked his father whether he wanted to have a beer and gladly offered to fetch it herself, and when his father was silent, she said, in order to remove any reservations he might have, that she could send the caretaker's wife to get it. But then the father would finally say a resounding "No," and nothing more would be spoken about it.

Already during the first day his father laid out all the financial circumstances and prospects to his mother and to his sister as well. From time to time he stood up from the table and pulled out of the small lockbox salvaged from his business, which had collapsed five years previously, some document or other or some notebook. The sound was audible as he opened up the complicated lock and, after removing what he was looking for, locked it up again. Some of the father's explanations were the first enjoyable thing that Gregor had the chance to listen to since his imprisonment began. He had thought that his father had been left with nothing at all from that business; at least his father had told him nothing to contradict that view, and Gregor in any case had not asked him about it. At the time Gregor's only concern had been to do everything he could in order to allow his family to forget as quickly as possible the business misfortune which had brought them all into a state of complete hopelessness. And so at that point he had started to work with a special intensity; from a minor assistant he had become, almost overnight, a traveling salesman, who naturally had entirely different possibilities for earning money and whose successes at work were converted immediately into the form of cash commissions, which could be set out on the table at home for his astonished and delighted family. Those had been beautiful days, and they had never come back since, at least not with the same splendor, in spite of the

pt. ends p. 41

fact that Gregor later earned so much money that he was in a position to bear the expenses of the entire family, costs which he, in fact, did bear. They had become quite accustomed to it, both the family and Gregor as well. They took the money with thanks, and he happily surrendered it, but there was no longer any special warmth about it. Only his sister had remained still close to Gregor, and it was his secret plan to send her next year to the Conservatory, regardless of the great expense which that necessarily involved and which would be made up in other ways. In contrast to Gregor, she loved music very much and knew how to play the violin charmingly. Now and then during Gregor's short stays in the city the Conservatory was mentioned in conversations with his sister, but always merely as a beautiful dream, whose realization was unimaginable; their parents never listened to these innocent expectations with pleasure. But Gregor thought about them with scrupulous consideration and intended to announce his proposal solemnly on Christmas Eve.

In his present situation, such completely futile ideas would go through his head while he pushed himself right up against the door and listened. Sometimes in his general exhaustion he could not listen anymore and let his head bang listlessly against the door, but he immediately pulled himself together once more, for even the small sound which he made by this motion would be heard nearby and silence everyone. "There he goes on again," his father would say after a while, clearly turning toward the door, and only then would the interrupted conversation gradually be resumed again.

Gregor soon found out clearly enough—for his father tended to repeat himself from time to time in his explanations, partly because he had not personally concerned himself with these matters for a long time now, and partly because his mother did not understand everything right away the first time—that, in spite of all bad luck, an amount of money, although a very small one, was still available from the old times and that the interest, which had not been touched, had in the intervening time accumulated a little. In addition to this, the money which Gregor had brought home every month—he had kept only a few crowns[3] for himself—had not been completely spent and had grown into a small capital amount. Gregor, behind his door, nodded eagerly, rejoicing over this unanticipated foresight and frugality. True, with this excess money, he could really have paid off more of the father's debt to his employer and the day on which he could be rid of this position would have been a lot closer, but now things were doubtless better the way his father had arranged them.

At the moment, however, this money was not nearly sufficient to permit the family to live off the interest payments. Perhaps the savings would be enough to maintain the family for one or at most two years, that was all. Thus, it only really added up to an amount that one should not draw upon and that should be set aside for an emergency. They had to earn money to live on. Now, it's true his father was indeed a healthy man, but he was old and had not worked for five years and thus could not be counted on for very much. He had in these five years, the first holidays of his laborious but unsuccessful life, put on a good deal of fat and thus had become really heavy. And should his old mother now be expected to work for money? A woman who suffered from asthma, for whom wandering through the apartment was even now a great strain and who spent every second day on the sofa by the open window, having trouble with her breathing? Should his sister earn money, a girl who was still a seventeen-year-old child and whose earlier lifestyle—consisting of dressing herself nicely, sleeping in late, helping around the house, taking part in a few modest enjoyments and, above all, playing the violin—had been so very delightful? When it came to talking about this need to earn money, Gregor would at first always let go of the door and throw himself on the cool leather sofa nearby, quite hot from shame and sorrow.

---

[3] Coins; money.

Often he lay there all night long, not sleeping at all, just scratching on the leather for hours at a time. Or he would take on the very difficult task of pushing a chair over to the window. Then he would creep up on the window sill and, braced on the chair, lean against the window to look out, obviously with some memory or other of the liberating sense which looking out the window used to bring him in earlier times. For, in fact, from day to day he perceived things with less and less clarity, even things that were only a short distance away. The hospital across the street, the all-too-frequent sight of which he had previously cursed, was not visible at all anymore, and if he had not been very well aware that he lived in the quiet but completely urban Charlotte Street, he could have believed that from his window he was peering out at a featureless wasteland, in which the gray heaven and the gray earth had merged and were indistinguishable. His observant sister had only to notice a couple of times that the chair stood by the window; then, after cleaning up the room, she would each time push the chair back right against the window again. She even began to leave the inner casements open.

If Gregor had only been able to speak to his sister and thank her for everything that she had to do for him, he would have tolerated her service more easily. As it was, he suffered under it. To her credit, the sister sought to cover up the awkwardness of everything as much as possible, and, as time went by, she naturally became more successful at it. But with the passing of time Gregor also came to understand everything much more clearly. Even the way she would come in was terrible for him. As soon as she entered, she ran straight to the window, without taking the time to shut the door—in spite of the fact that at other times she was very careful to spare anyone the sight of Gregor's room—and yanked the window open with eager hands, as if she were almost suffocating, and remained for a while by the window breathing deeply, even when it was very cold. With all her noisy rushing about she frightened Gregor twice every day. The entire time he trembled under the couch, and yet he knew very well that she would certainly have spared him all this gladly if it had only been possible for her to remain with the window closed in a room where Gregor lived.

On one occasion—about one month had already gone by since Gregor's transformation, and there was no particular reason any more for his sister to be startled at Gregor's appearance—she arrived a little earlier than usual and came upon Gregor as he was still looking out the window, immobile and positioned as if to frighten someone. It would not have come as a surprise to Gregor if she had not come in, since his position was preventing her from opening the window immediately. But not only did she not step inside; she even stepped back and shut the door. A stranger really could have concluded from this that Gregor had been lying in wait for her and wanted to bite her. Of course, Gregor immediately concealed himself under the couch, but he had to wait until noon before his sister returned, and she seemed much less calm than usual. From this he realized that his appearance was still intolerable to her and should remain intolerable to her in future—and that she really must have to exert a lot of self-control not to run away from a glimpse of only the small part of his body which stuck out from under the couch. In order to spare her even this sight, one day he dragged the bedsheet on his back up onto the couch—this task took him four hours—and arranged it in such a way that he was now completely concealed and his sister, even if she bent down, could not see him. If this sheet was not necessary as far as she was concerned, then she could certainly have removed it, for it was clear enough that Gregor could not derive any pleasure from isolating himself away so completely. But she left the sheet just as it was, and Gregor believed he even caught a look of gratitude when, on one occasion, he carefully lifted up the sheet a little with his head to check as his sister took stock of the new arrangement.

In the first two weeks his parents could not bring themselves to visit him, and he often heard how they fully acknowledged his sister's present work; whereas, earlier they had often got annoyed at his sister because she had seemed to them a somewhat useless girl. Now both his father and his mother frequently waited in front of Gregor's door while his sister cleaned up inside. As soon as she came out, she had to explain in great detail how things looked in the room, what Gregor had eaten, how he had behaved this time, and whether perhaps a slight improvement was perceptible. As it happened, his mother comparatively soon had wanted to visit Gregor, but his father and his sister had restrained her, at first with reasons which Gregor listened to very attentively and which he completely endorsed. Later, however, they had to hold her back forcefully. When she then cried "Let me go to Gregor. He's my unfortunate son! Don't you understand that I have to go to him?" Gregor then thought that perhaps it would be a good thing if his mother came in, not every day, of course, but maybe once a week. She understood everything much better than his sister, who, in spite of all her courage, was still merely a child and, in the last analysis, had perhaps undertaken such a difficult task only out of childish recklessness.

Gregor's wish to see his mother was soon realized. While during the day Gregor, out of consideration for his parents, did not want to show himself by the window, he could not crawl around very much on the few square meters of the floor. He found it difficult to bear lying quietly during the night, and soon eating no longer gave him the slightest pleasure. So for diversion he acquired the habit of crawling back and forth across the walls and ceiling. He was especially fond of hanging from the ceiling. The experience was quite different from lying on the floor. It was easier to breathe, a slight vibration went through his body, and in the midst of the almost happy amusement which Gregor found up there, it could happen that, to his own surprise, he let go and hit the floor. However, now he naturally controlled his body quite differently than before, and he did not injure himself in such a great fall. Now, his sister noticed immediately the new amusement which Gregor had found for himself—for as he crept around he left behind here and there traces of his sticky stuff—and so she got the idea of making the area where Gregor could creep around as large as possible and thus of removing the furniture which got in the way, especially the chest of drawers and the writing desk. But she was in no position to do this by herself. She did not dare to ask her father to help, and the servant girl would certainly not have assisted her, for although this girl, about sixteen years old, had courageously remained since the dismissal of the previous cook, she had begged for the privilege of being allowed to stay permanently confined to the kitchen and of having to open the door only in answer to a special summons. Thus, his sister had no other choice but to involve his mother, choosing a time when his father was absent. His mother approached Gregor's room with cries of excited joy, but she fell silent at the door. Of course, his sister first checked whether everything in the room was in order. Only then did she let his mother enter. Gregor had, with the greatest haste, drawn the sheet down even further and wrinkled it more. The whole thing really looked just like a coverlet [4] thrown carelessly over the couch. On this occasion, Gregor also held back from spying out from under the sheet. For now, he refrained from looking at his mother and was merely happy that she had now come.

"Come on. You can't see him," said his sister and evidently led his mother by the hand. Now Gregor listened as these two weak women shifted the heavy old chest of drawers from its position. His sister constantly took on herself the greatest part of the work, without listening to the warnings of his mother, who was afraid that she would strain herself. The work lasted a very long time. After about a quarter of an hour had already gone by, his mother said it would be better if they left the chest of drawers where it was, because, in the first place, it was too heavy. They would not be finished before his father's arrival, and leaving the chest of drawers in the middle of the room would block all Gregor's pathways, but, in the second place, they could not be at all certain

---

[4] A bedspread, typically less than floor-length.

that Gregor would be pleased with the removal of the furniture. To Gregor's mother the reverse seemed likely to be true. The sight of the empty walls pierced her right to the heart; and why should Gregor not feel the same? He had been accustomed to the room furnishings for a long time and without them would feel himself abandoned in an empty room. "And is it not the case," his mother concluded very quietly, almost whispering, as if she wished to prevent Gregor, whose exact location she really did not know, from hearing even the sound of her voice—for she was convinced that he did not understand her words—"and isn't it a fact that by removing the furniture we'd be showing that we were giving up all hope of an improvement and leaving him to his own resources without any consideration? I think it would be best if we tried to keep the room exactly in the condition it was in before, so that, when Gregor returns to us, he finds everything unchanged and can forget the intervening time all the more easily."

As he heard his mother's words Gregor realized that the lack of all immediate human contact, together with the monotonous life surrounded by the family over the course of these two months, must have confused his understanding, because otherwise he could not explain to himself how he, in all seriousness, could have been so keen to have his room emptied. Was he really eager to let the warm room, comfortably furnished with pieces he had inherited, be turned into a cavern in which he would, of course, then be able to crawl about in all directions without disturbance, but at the same time with a quick and complete forgetting of his human past as well? Was he then at this point already on the verge of forgetting and was it only the voice of his mother, which he had not heard for a long time, that had aroused him? Nothing was to be removed—everything must remain. In his condition he could not function without the beneficial influences of his furniture. And if the furniture prevented him from carrying out his senseless crawling about all over the place, then there was no harm in that, but rather a great benefit.

But his sister unfortunately thought otherwise. She had grown accustomed, certainly not without justification, to acting as a special expert when discussing matters concerning Gregor with their parents, and so now the mother's advice was for his sister sufficient reason to insist on the removal, not only of the chest of drawers and the writing desk, which were the only items she had thought about at first, but also of all the rest of the furniture, with the exception of the indispensable couch. Of course, it was not only childish defiance and her recent very unexpected and hard won self-confidence which led her to this demand. She had also actually observed that Gregor needed a great deal of room to creep about; the furniture, on the other hand, as far as one could see, was not the slightest use. But perhaps the enthusiastic sensibility of young women of her age also played a role. This feeling sought release at every opportunity, and with it Grete now felt tempted by the desire to make Gregor's situation even more terrifying, so that then she would be able to do even more for him than she had up to now. For surely no one except Grete would ever trust themselves to enter a room in which Gregor ruled the empty walls all by himself.

And so she did not let herself be dissuaded from her decision by her mother, who in her sheer agitation seemed uncertain of herself in the room as it was. She soon fell quiet, and helped his sister with all the energy she could muster to get the chest of drawers out of the room. Now, Gregor could still do without the chest of drawers if need be, but the writing desk really had to stay. And scarcely had the women left the room with the chest of drawers, groaning as they pushed it, when Gregor stuck his head out from under the sofa to see how he could intervene, cautiously and with as much consideration as possible. But unfortunately it was his mother who came back into the room first; Grete had her arms wrapped around the chest of drawers in the next room and was rocking it back and forth by herself, of course without moving it from its position. But his mother was not used to the sight of Gregor; just seeing him could have made her ill, and so, frightened, Gregor scurried backward right to the other end of

pt. ends p. 41

the sofa. However, he could no longer prevent the front of the sheet from moving a little. That was enough to catch his mother's attention. She came to a halt, stood still for a moment, and then went back to Grete.

Although Gregor kept repeating to himself over and over that really nothing unusual was going on, that only a few pieces of furniture were being rearranged, he soon had to admit to himself that the movements of the women to and fro, their quiet conversations, and the scraping of the furniture on the floor affected him like a great commotion stirred up on all sides. He was pulling in his head and legs and pressing his body into the floor so firmly that he had to tell himself unequivocally he would not be able to endure all this much longer. They were cleaning out his room, taking away from him everything he cherished; they had already dragged out the chest of drawers in which the fretsaw[5] and other tools were kept, and they were now loosening the writing desk which was fixed tight to the floor, the desk on which he, as a business student, as a high school student, indeed even as an elementary school student, had written out his assignments. At that moment he really did not have any more time to consider the good intentions of the two women, whose existence he had in any case almost forgotten, because in their exhaustion they were working really silently; the heavy stumbling of their feet was the only sound to be heard.

And so he scuttled out—the women were just propping themselves up on the writing desk in the next room in order to take a short breather. He changed the direction of his path four times. He really did not know what he should rescue first. Then he saw hanging conspicuously on an otherwise empty wall the picture of the woman dressed in nothing but fur. He quickly scurried up over it and pressed himself against the glass which held it in place and which made his hot abdomen feel good. At least this picture, which Gregor for the moment completely concealed—surely

---

[5] A saw with a narrow blade stretched vertically on a frame, for cutting thin wood in patterns.

no one would now take this away. He twisted his head toward the door of the living room to observe the women as they came back in.

They had not allowed themselves very much rest and were coming back right away. Grete had placed her arm around her mother and held her tightly. "So what shall we take now?" said Grete and looked around her. Then her glance met Gregor's from the wall. She kept her composure only because her mother was there. She bent her face toward her mother in order to prevent her from looking around, and said, although in a trembling voice and too quickly, "Come, wouldn't it be better to go back to the living room for just another moment?" Grete's purpose was clear to Gregor: she wanted to take his mother to a safe place and then chase him down from the wall. Well, let her just try! He squatted on his picture and did not hand it over. He would sooner spring into Grete's face.

But Grete's words had immediately made the mother very uneasy. She walked to the side, caught sight of the enormous brown splotch on the flowered wallpaper, and, before she became truly aware that what she was looking at was Gregor, screamed out in a high-pitched raw voice "Oh God, oh God" and fell with outstretched arms, as if she was surrendering everything, down onto the couch. She lay there motionless.

"Gregor, you . . ." cried out his sister with a raised fist and an urgent glare. Since his transformation these were the first words she had directed right at him. She ran into the room next door to bring some spirits—anything with which she could revive her mother from her fainting spell. Gregor wanted to help as well—there was time enough to save the picture—but he was stuck fast on the glass and had to tear himself loose forcibly. Then he too scurried into the next room, as if he could give his sister some advice, as in earlier times. He had to stand there idly behind her, while she rummaged about among various small bottles. Still, she was frightened when she turned around. A bottle fell onto the floor and shattered. A splinter of glass wounded Gregor in

pt. ends p. 41

the face, and some corrosive medicine or other dripped over him. Now, without lingering any longer, Grete took as many small bottles as she could hold and ran with them in to her mother. She slammed the door shut with her foot. Gregor was now shut off from his mother, who was perhaps near death, thanks to him. He could not open the door; he did not want to chase away his sister, who had to remain with the mother. At this point he had nothing to do but wait. Overwhelmed with self-reproach and worry, he began to creep and crawl over everything: walls, furniture, and ceiling. Finally, in his despair, as the entire room started to spin around him, he fell onto the middle of the large table.

A short time elapsed. Gregor lay there limply. All around was still. Perhaps that was a good sign. Then there was a ring at the door. The servant girl was naturally shut up in her kitchen, and therefore Grete had to go to open the door. His father had arrived.

"What's happened?" were his first words. Grete's appearance had told him everything. Grete replied with a dull voice; evidently she was pressing her face against her father's chest: "Mother fainted, but she's getting better now. Gregor has broken loose."

"Yes, I expected that," said his father, "I always warned you of that, but you women don't want to listen."

It was clear to Gregor that the father had badly misunderstood Grete's all-too-brief message and was assuming that Gregor had committed some violent crime or other. Thus, Gregor now had to find his father to calm him down, for he had neither the time nor the ability to explain things to him. And so he rushed away to the door of his room and pushed himself against it, so that his father could see right away as he entered from the hall that Gregor fully intended to return at once to his room, that it was not necessary to drive him back, but that one only needed to open the door, and he would disappear immediately.

But his father was not in the mood to observe such niceties. "Ah!" he yelled as soon as he entered, with a tone as if he were at once angry and pleased. Gregor pulled his head back from the door and raised it in the direction of his father. He had not really pictured his father as he now stood there. Of course, what with his new style of creeping all around, he had in the past while neglected to pay attention to what was going on in the rest of the apartment, as he had used to do; he really should have grasped the fact that he would encounter different conditions. And yet, and yet, was that still his father? Was that the same man who had lain exhausted and buried in bed in earlier days when Gregor was setting out on a business trip; who had received him on the evenings of his return in a sleeping gown and arm chair, totally incapable of standing up; who had only lifted his arms as a sign of happiness; and who in their rare strolls together a few Sundays a year and on the most important holidays made his way slowly forward between Gregor and his mother—who themselves moved slowly—even a bit more slowly than them, bundled up in his old coat, working hard to move forward and always setting down his walking stick carefully; and who, when he had wanted to say something, had almost always stood still and gathered his entourage around him? Now he was standing up really straight, dressed in a tight-fitting blue uniform with gold buttons, like the ones doormen wear in a banking company. Above the high stiff collar of his jacket his firm double chin stuck out prominently, beneath his bushy eyebrows the glance of his black eyes was fresh and alert, and his usually disheveled white hair was combed down into a shining and carefully exact part. He threw his cap, on which a gold monogram, probably the symbol of a bank, was affixed, in an arc across the entire room onto the sofa and, thrusting back the edges of the long coat of his uniform, with his hands in his trouser pockets and a grim face, moved right up to Gregor. He really did not know what he had in mind, but he raised his feet uncommonly high anyway, and Gregor was astonished at the gigantic size of the soles of his boots. Gregor did not linger on that point; he had known even from the first day of his new life that, as far as he was concerned, his father considered the only appropriate response to be the most forceful one. And so he scurried away from his father, stopped when his father remained standing, and scampered forward again when his father stirred a little. In this way they made their way around the room repeatedly, without anything decisive taking place. In fact, because of the slow pace, it did not look like a chase. Gregor remained on the floor for the time being, especially since he was afraid that his father could interpret a flight up onto the wall or the ceiling as an act of real malice. At any event, Gregor had to tell himself that he could not keep up this running around for a long time, because whenever his father took a single step, he had to go through a large number of movements. Already he was starting to feel short of breath, just as in his earlier days when his lungs had been quite unreliable. As he now staggered around in this way, trying to gather all his energy for running, hardly able to keep his eyes open and feeling so listless that he had no notion at all of any escape other than by running and had almost already forgotten that the walls were available to him, although here they were obstructed by carefully carved furniture full of sharp points and spikes—at that moment something or other thrown casually flew close by and rolled in front of him. It was an apple. Immediately a second one flew after it. Gregor stood still in fright. Further running away was useless, for his father had decided to bombard him. From the fruit bowl on the sideboard his father had filled his pockets, and now, without for the moment taking accurate aim, he was throwing apple after apple. These small red apples were rolling around on the floor, as if electrified, and colliding with each other. A weakly thrown apple grazed Gregor's back but skidded off harmlessly. However, another thrown immediately after that one drove into his back really hard. Gregor wanted to drag himself onward, as if he could make the unexpected and incredible pain go away if he changed his position. But he felt as if he was nailed in place and lay stretched out, completely confused in all his senses. Only with his final glance did he notice how the door of his room was pulled open; and how, right in front of his screaming sister, his mother ran out in her underbodice (for his sister had loosened her clothing in order to give her some freedom to breathe in her fainting spell); and how his mother then ran up to his father—on the way her loosened petticoats slipping toward the floor one after the other[6]—and how, tripping over them, she hurled herself onto the father and, throwing her arms around him, in complete union with him—but at this moment Gregor's powers of sight gave way—as her hands reached around the father's neck, and she begged him to spare Gregor's life.

[6] An underbodice and petticoats are both light, loose undergarments.

III

Gregor's serious wound, from which he suffered for over a month—since no one ventured to remove the apple, it remained in his flesh as a visible reminder—seemed by itself to have reminded the father that, in spite of Gregor's present unhappy and hateful appearance, he was a member of the family and should not be treated as an enemy. It was, on the contrary, a requirement of family duty to suppress one's aversion and to endure—nothing else, just endure.

If, through his wound, Gregor had now also apparently lost for good his ability to move and for the time being needed many, many minutes to crawl across his room, like an aged invalid—so far as creeping up high was concerned, that was unimaginable—nevertheless, for this worsening of his condition, in his view he did get completely satisfactory compensation, because everyday toward evening the door to the living room, which he was in the habit of keeping a sharp eye on even one or two hours beforehand, was opened, so that he, lying down in the darkness of his room, invisible from the living room, could see the entire family at the illuminated table and listen to their conversation, to a certain extent with their common permission, a situation quite different from what had happened before.

Of course, it was no longer the animated social interaction of former times—of the sort which Gregor had always thought about with a certain longing in small hotel rooms, when, tired out, he had had to throw himself into the damp bedclothes. For the most part what went on now was only very quiet. After the evening meal, the father soon fell asleep in his armchair. The mother and sister warned each other to be quiet. Bent far over the light, the mother sewed fine undergarments for a fashion shop. The sister, who had taken on a job as a salesgirl, in the evening studied stenography and French, so as perhaps to obtain a better position later on. Sometimes the father woke up and, as if he was quite ignorant that he had been asleep, said to the mother "How long you have been sewing again today!" and went right back to sleep, while the mother and the sister smiled tiredly to each other.

With a sort of stubbornness the father refused to take off his servant's uniform even at home, and while his sleeping gown hung unused on the coat hook, the father dozed completely dressed in his place, as if he was always ready for his responsibility and even here was waiting for the voice of his superior. As a result, in spite of all the care from the mother and sister, his uniform, which even at the start was not new, grew dirty, and Gregor looked, often for the entire evening, at this clothing, with stains all over it and with its gold buttons always polished, in which the old man, though he must have been very uncomfortable, nonetheless was sleeping peacefully.

As soon as the clock struck ten, the mother tried gently to encourage the father to wake up and then to persuade him to go to bed, on the grounds that he could not get a proper sleep here and that the father, who had to report for service at six o'clock, really needed a good sleep. But in his stubbornness, which had gripped him since he had become an employee, he always insisted on staying even longer by the table, although he regularly fell asleep and then could be prevailed upon only with the greatest difficulty to trade his chair for the bed. No matter how much the mother and sister might at that point work on him with small admonitions, for a quarter of an hour he would remain shaking his head slowly, his eyes closed, without standing up. The mother would pull him by the sleeve and speak flattering words into his ear; the sister would leave her work to help her mother, but that would not have the desired effect on the father. He would merely settle himself even more deeply into his arm chair. Only when the two women grabbed him under the armpits would he throw his eyes open, look back and forth at the mother and sister, and habitually say, "This is a life. This is the peace and quiet of my old age." And propped up by both women, he would heave himself up elaborately, as if for him it was the greatest trouble, allow himself to be led to the door by the women, wave them away, and proceed on his own from that point, while the mother quickly threw down her sewing implements and the sister her pen in order to run after the father and help him some more.

In this overworked and exhausted family who had time any longer to worry about Gregor more than was absolutely necessary? The household was constantly getting smaller. The servant girl had been let go. A huge bony cleaning woman with white hair flying all over her head now came in the morning and evening to do the heaviest work. The mother took care of everything else, in addition to her considerable sewing work. It even happened that various pieces of family jewelery, which previously the mother and sister had been overjoyed to wear on social and festive occasions, were sold, as Gregor found out in the evening from the general discussion of the prices they had fetched. But the greatest complaint was always that they could not leave this apartment, which was much too big for their present means, since it was impossible to imagine how Gregor might be moved. Gregor fully recognized that it was not just consideration for him which was preventing a move, for he could have been transported easily in a suitable box with a few air holes. The main thing holding the family back from a change in living quarters was far more their complete hopelessness and the idea that they had been struck by a misfortune like no one else in their entire circle of relatives and acquaintances. What the world demands of poor

pt. ends p. 62

people they now carried out to an extreme degree. The father brought breakfast to the petty officials at the bank; the mother sacrificed herself for the undergarments of strangers; the sister behind her desk was at the beck and call of customers. But the family's energies did not extend any further. And the wound in Gregor's back began to pain him all over again, when his mother and sister, after they had escorted the father to bed, now came back, let their work lie, moved close together, and sat cheek to cheek and when his mother would now say, pointing to Gregor's room, "Close the door, Grete," and when Gregor was again in the darkness, while close by the women mingled their tears or, quite dry-eyed, stared at the table.

Gregor spent his nights and days with hardly any sleep. Sometimes he thought that the next time the door opened he would take over the family arrangements just as he had earlier. In his imagination appeared again, after a long time, his boss and the manager, the chief clerk and the apprentices, the excessively dense custodian, two or three friends from other businesses, a chambermaid from a hotel in the provinces (a loving, fleeting memory), a cashier from a hat shop, whom he had seriously but too slowly courted—they all appeared mixed in with strangers or people he had already forgotten, but instead of helping him and his family, they were all unapproachable, and he was happy to see them disappear. But sometimes he was in no mood to worry about his family. He could be filled with sheer anger over the wretched care he was getting, even though he could not imagine anything which he might have an appetite for. Still, he made plans about how he could get into the pantry to take there what he at all accounts deserved, even if he was not hungry. Without thinking any more about what might give Gregor special plea-sure, the sister very quickly kicked some food or other, whatever she felt like, into his room in the morning and at noon, before she ran off to her shop. And in the evening, quite indifferent to whether the food had perhaps only been tasted or—what happened most frequently—remained entirely undisturbed, she whisked it out with one sweep of her broom. The task of clean-ing his room, which she now always carried out in the evening, could not have been done any more quickly. Streaks of dirt ran along the walls; here and there lay tangles of dust and garbage. At first, when his sister arrived, Gregor positioned himself in a particularly filthy corner as a way of making some sort of pro-test. But he could well have stayed there for weeks without his sister's doing the job any better. In fact, she saw the dirt as well as he did, but she had decided just to let it stay. In this business, with a touchiness which was quite new to her and which had generally taken over the entire family, she kept watch to see that the cleaning of Gregor's room remained reserved for her. His mother had once undertaken a major cleanup of his room, which she had only completed successfully after using a few buckets of water. The extensive dampness made Gregor sick, however, and he lay spread out, embittered and immobile, on the couch. But the mother did not escape punishment. For in the evening the sister had hardly observed the change in Gregor's room before she ran into the living room mightily offended and, in spite of her mother's hand lifted high in entreaty, broke out in a fit of crying. Her parents—the father had, of course, woken up with a start in his armchair—at first looked at her astonished and helpless, but then they started to get agitated as well. Turning to his right, the father heaped reproaches on the mother that she had not left the cleaning of Gregor's room to the sister and, turning to his left, he shouted at the sister that she would never again be allowed to clean Gregor's room, while the mother tried to pull the father, beside himself in his excitement, into the bedroom. The sister, shaken by her crying fit, pounded on the table with her tiny fists, and Gregor hissed at all this, angry that no one thought about shutting the door and sparing him the sight of this commotion.

But even when the sister, exhausted from her daily work, had grown tired of caring for Gregor as she had before, even then the mother did not have to come at all in her place. And Gregor did not have to be neglected. For now the cleaning woman was there. This old widow, whose strong bony frame had enabled her to survive the worst a long life can offer, had no real horror of Gregor. Without being in the least curious, she had once accidentally opened Gregor's door. At the sight of Gregor, who, totally surprised, began to scamper here and there, although no one was chasing him, she remained standing with her hands folded across her stomach staring at him. Since then she would never fail to open the door furtively a little every morning and evening and look in on Gregor. At first, she also called him to her with words that she probably thought were friendly, like "Come on over here, old dung beetle!" or "Hey, look at the old dung beetle!" Addressed in such a manner, Gregor made no answer, but remained motionless in his place, as if the door had not been opened at all. If only, instead of allowing this cleaning woman to disturb him uselessly whenever she felt like it, they had given her orders to clean up his room everyday! Once in the early morning—a hard downpour, perhaps already a sign of the coming spring, struck the windowpanes—when the cleaning woman started up once again with her usual conversation, Gregor was so bitter that he turned toward her, as if for an attack, although slowly and weakly. But instead of being afraid of him, the cleaning woman merely lifted up a chair standing close by the door and, as she stood there with her mouth wide open, her intention was clear: she would close her mouth only when the chair in her hand had been thrown down on Gregor's back. "This goes no further, all right?" she asked, as Gregor turned himself around again, and she placed the chair calmly back in the corner.

Gregor ate hardly anything anymore. Only when he chanced to move past the food which had been prepared did he, as a game, take a bit into his mouth, hold it there for hours, and generally spit it out again. At first he thought it might be his sadness over the condition of his room that kept him from eating, but he very soon became reconciled to the alterations in his room. People had grown accustomed to discard in there things which they could not put anywhere else, and at this point there were many such items, now that they had rented one room of the apartment to three lodgers. These solemn gentlemen—all three had full beards, as Gregor once found out through a crack in the door—were meticulously intent on tidiness, not only in their own room but, since they had now rented a room here, in the entire household, particularly in the kitchen. They simply did not tolerate any useless, let alone any dirty, stuff. Moreover, for the most part they had brought with them their own pieces of furniture. Thus, many items had become superfluous, but these were not really things one could sell or things people wanted to throw out. All these pieces ended up in Gregor's room, even the box of ashes and the garbage pail from the kitchen. The cleaning woman, always in a great hurry, simply flung anything that was for the moment useless into Gregor's room. Fortunately Gregor generally saw only the relevant object and the hand which held it. The cleaning woman perhaps was intending, when time and opportunity allowed, to take the stuff out again or to throw everything out all at once, but in fact the things remained lying there, wherever they had ended up at the first throw, unless Gregor squirmed his way through the accumulation of junk and moved them. At first he was forced to do this because otherwise there was no room for him to creep around; later he did it with a growing pleasure, although after such movements, tired to death and feeling wretched, he did not budge again for hours.

Because the lodgers sometimes also took their evening meal at home in the common living room, the door to it stayed shut on many evenings. But Gregor had no trouble at all going without the open door. Already on many evenings when it was open he had not availed himself of it, but, without the family noticing, was stretched out in the darkest corner of his room. However, on one occasion the cleaning woman had left the door to the living room slightly ajar, and it remained open even when the lodgers came in, as evening fell and the lights were put on. They sat down at the head of the table—where in earlier days the mother,

pt. ends p. 62

the father, and Gregor had eaten—unfolded their serviettes,[1] and picked up their knives and forks. The mother immediately appeared in the door with a dish of meat and right behind her the sister with a dish piled high with potatoes. The food gave off a lot of steam. The gentlemen lodgers bent over the plates set before them, as if they wanted to check them before eating, and in fact the one who sat in the middle—for the other two he seemed to serve as the authority—cut off a piece of meat still on the serving dish, obviously to establish whether it was sufficiently tender and whether or not it should be sent back to the kitchen. He was satisfied, and mother and sister, who had looked on in suspense, began to breathe easily and to smile.

The family itself ate in the kitchen. In spite of that, before the father went into the kitchen, he came into the living room and with a single bow, cap in hand, made a tour of the table. The lodgers rose up collectively and murmured something into their beards. Then, when they were alone, they ate almost in complete silence. It seemed odd to Gregor that, out of all the many different sorts of sounds of eating, what was always audible was their chewing teeth, as if by that Gregor should be shown that people needed their teeth to eat and that nothing could be done even with the most handsome toothless jawbone. "I really do have an appetite," Gregor said to himself sorrowfully, "but not for these things. How these lodgers stuff themselves, and I am dying of hunger!"

On this very evening the violin sounded from the kitchen. Gregor did not remember ever hearing it all through this period. The lodgers had already ended their night meal, the middle one had pulled out a newspaper and had given each of the other two a page, and they were now leaning back, reading and smoking. When the violin started playing, they became attentive, got up, and went on tiptoe to the hall door, at which they remained standing pressed up against one another.

---

[1] Napkins.

They must have been audible from the kitchen, because Gregor's father called out, "Perhaps the gentlemen don't like the playing? It can be stopped at once."

"On the contrary," stated the lodger in the middle, "might the young woman not come in to us and play in the room here, where it is really much more comfortable and cheerful?"

"Oh, certainly," cried Gregor's father, as if he were the one playing the violin. The men stepped back into the room and waited. Soon his father came with the music stand, his mother with the sheet music, and his sister with the violin. His sister calmly prepared everything for the recital. His parents, who had never previously rented a room and therefore behaved with exaggerated politeness to the lodgers, dared not sit on their own chairs. His father leaned against the door, his right hand stuck between two buttons of his buttoned-up uniform. His mother, however, accepted a chair offered by one of the lodgers. Since she let the chair stay where the gentleman had chanced to put it, she sat to one side in a corner.

His sister began to play. His father and mother, one on each side, followed attentively the movements of her hands. Attracted by the playing, Gregor had ventured to advance a little further forward, and his head was already in the living room. He scarcely wondered about the fact that recently he had had so little consideration for the others. Earlier, consideration for his family had been something he was proud of. And for that very reason he would have had at this moment more reason to hide away, because as a result of the dust which lay all over his room and flew around with the slightest movement, he was totally covered in dirt. On his back and his sides he carted around with him threads, hair, and remnants of food. His indifference to everything was much too great for him to lie on his back and scour himself on the carpet, as he had done earlier several times a day. Now, in spite of his condition he had no timidity about inching forward a bit on the spotless floor of the living room.

In any case, no one paid him any attention. The family was

all caught up in the violin playing. The lodgers, by contrast, having initially placed themselves, hands in their trouser pockets, behind the music stand much too close to his sister, so that they could all see the sheet music, something that must certainly have bothered his sister, soon drew back to the window conversing in low voices with bowed heads, where they then remained, anxiously observed by the father. It now seemed abundantly clear that, having assumed they were to hear a beautiful or entertaining violin recital, they were disappointed; they had had enough of the entire performance and were allowing their peace and quiet to be disturbed only out of politeness. In particular, the way in which they all blew the smoke from their cigars out of their noses and mouths up into the air led one to conclude that they were very tense. And yet his sister was playing so beautifully. Her face was turned to the side, her eyes following the score intently and sadly. Gregor crept forward still a little further, keeping his head close against the floor in order to be able to catch her gaze if possible. Was he a beast that music so captivated him? It was as if the way to the unknown nourishment he craved was revealing itself. He was determined to press forward right up to his sister, to tug at her dress, and to indicate to her in this way that she might still come with her violin into his room, because here no one valued the recital as he longed to value it. He did not wish to let her go from his room anymore, at least not while he was still alive. His frightening appearance would for the first time become useful for him. He wanted to be at all the doors of his room simultaneously and snarl back at the attackers. However, his sister should not be compelled but would remain with him voluntarily. She would sit next to him on the sofa, bend down her ear to him, and he would then confide in her that he had firmly intended to send her to the Conservatory and that, if his misfortune had not arrived in the interim, he would have declared all this last Christmas—had Christmas really already come and gone?—and would have brooked[2] no argument. After this explanation his sister would break out in tears of emotion, and Gregor would lift himself up to her shoulder and kiss her throat, which she, from the time she had been going to work, had left exposed without a ribbon or a collar.

"Mr. Samsa!" called out the middle lodger to the father and, without uttering a further word, pointed his index finger at Gregor as he was moving slowly forward. The violin fell silent. The middle lodger smiled, first shaking his head at his friends, and then looked down at Gregor once more. Rather than driving Gregor back, his father seemed to consider it more important for the time being to calm down the lodgers, although they were not at all upset and Gregor seemed to entertain them more than the violin recital. His father hurried over to them and with outstretched arms tried to push them into their own room and at the same time to block their view of Gregor with his own body. At this point they really did become somewhat irritated, although it was hard to tell whether that was because of his father's behavior or because of the knowledge they had just acquired—that they had a neighbor like Gregor and had not been aware of it. They demanded explanations from his father, raised their arms to make their points, tugged agitatedly at their beards, and moved back toward their room quite slowly. In the meantime, his sister, suddenly left on her own, had felt overwhelmed by the unexpected breaking off of the recital. She had held onto the violin and bow in her limp hands for a little while and had continued to look at the sheet music as if she were still playing. All at once she pulled herself together, placed the instrument in her mother's lap—the mother was still sitting in her chair having trouble breathing, her lungs laboring hard—and had run into the next room, which the lodgers, pressured by the father, were already approaching more rapidly. One could observe how under his sister's practiced hands the covers and pillows on the beds

[2] Tolerated or allowed.

were thrown high and then rearranged. Even before the lodgers had reached the room, she had finished fixing the beds and was slipping out. His father seemed once again so gripped by his stubbornness that he forgot about the respect that, after all, he must show his lodgers. He pressed on and on, until right in the door of the room the middle gentleman stamped loudly with his foot and thus brought Gregor's father to a standstill. "I hereby declare," the middle lodger said, raising his hand and casting his glance both on Gregor's mother and sister, "that considering the disgraceful conditions prevailing in this apartment and family"— with this he spat decisively on the floor—"I immediately cancel my room. I will, of course, pay nothing at all for the days which I have lived here; on the contrary, I shall think about whether or not I will initiate some sort of action against you, something which—believe me—would be very easy to establish." He fell silent and looked directly in front of him, as if he was waiting for something. In fact, his two friends immediately joined in with their opinions, "We also give immediate notice." At that he seized the door handle and with a bang slammed the door shut.

Gregor's father groped his way tottering to his chair and let himself fall into it. It looked as if he were stretching out for his usual evening snooze, but the heavy nodding of his head, which appeared as if it had no support, showed that he was not sleeping at all. Gregor had lain motionless the entire time in the spot where the lodgers had caught him out. Disappointment with the collapse of his plan and perhaps also weakness brought on by his severe hunger made it impossible for him to move. He was afraid and reasonably certain that they might launch a combined attack against him at any moment, and he waited. He was not even startled when the violin fell from his mother's lap, out from under her trembling fingers, and gave off a reverberating tone.

"My dear parents," said his sister, banging her hand on the table by way of an introduction, "things cannot go on any longer in this way. If you don't understand that, well, I do. I will not utter my brother's name in front of this monster, and thus I say only that we must try to get rid of it. We have tried what is humanly possible to take care of it and to be patient. I believe that no one can criticize us in the slightest."

"She is right in a thousand ways," said his father to himself. His mother, who was still incapable of breathing properly, began to cough numbly with her hand held up over her mouth and a manic expression in her eyes.

His sister hurried over to her mother and held her forehead. His sister's words seemed to have led his father to certain reflections. He sat upright, played with his service hat among the plates, which still lay on the table from the lodgers' evening meal, and looked now and then at the motionless Gregor.

"We must try to get rid of it," his sister now said decisively to his father, for his mother, in her coughing fit, was not listening to anything. "It is killing you both. I see it coming. When people have to work as hard as we all do, they can't also tolerate this endless torment at home. I just can't go on anymore." And she broke out into such a crying fit that her tears flowed down onto her mother's face. She wiped them off her mother with mechanical motions of her hands.

"Child," said her father sympathetically and with obvious appreciation, "then what should we do?"

Gregor's sister only shrugged her shoulders as a sign of the perplexity which, in contrast to her previous confidence, had now come over her while she was crying.

"If he understood us," said his father in a half-questioning tone. His sister, in the midst of her sobbing, shook her hand energetically as a sign that there was no point thinking of that.

"If he understood us," repeated his father and by shutting his eyes he absorbed the sister's conviction of the impossibility of this point, "then perhaps some compromise would be possible with him. But as it is . . . "

"It has to go," cried his sister. "That is the only way, Father. You must try to get rid of the idea that this is Gregor. The fact that we have believed this for so long, that is our real misfortune.

pt. ends p. 62

But how can it be Gregor? If it were Gregor, he would have long ago realized that a life among human beings is not possible for such a creature and would have gone away voluntarily. Then we would not have a brother, but we could go on living and honor his memory. But this animal plagues us. It drives away the lodgers and obviously wants to take over the entire apartment and leave us to spend the night in the alley. Just look, father," she suddenly cried out, "he's already starting up again." With a fright which was totally incomprehensible to Gregor, his sister left his mother, literally pushed herself away from her chair, as if she would sooner sacrifice her mother than remain in Gregor's vicinity, and rushed behind her father who, excited merely by her behavior, also stood up and half raised his arms in front of Gregor's sister as though to protect her.

But Gregor did not have any notion of wishing to create problems for anyone and certainly not for his sister. He had just started to turn himself around in order to creep back into his room, quite a startling sight, since, as a result of his ailing condition, he had to guide himself through the difficulty of turning around with his head, in this process lifting and striking it against the floor several times. He paused and looked around. His good intentions seemed to have been recognized. The fright had lasted only for a moment. Now they looked at him in silence and sorrow. His mother lay in her chair, with her legs stretched out and pressed together, her eyes almost shut from weariness. His father and sister sat next to one another. His sister had laid her hand around her father's neck.

"Now perhaps I can actually turn myself around," thought Gregor and began the task again. He couldn't stop puffing at the effort and had to rest now and then. No one was urging him on; it was all left to him on his own. When he had finished turning around, he immediately began to head straight back toward his room. He was astonished at the great distance which separated him from his room and did not understand in the least how in his weakness he had covered the same distance a short time before, almost without noticing it. Always intent only on creeping along quickly, he hardly paid any attention to the fact that no word or cry from his family interrupted him. Only when he was already in the doorway did he turn his head, not completely, because he felt his neck growing stiff. At any rate, he still saw that behind him nothing had changed. Only his sister was standing up. His last glimpse brushed over his mother, who was now completely asleep.

He was only just inside his room when the door was pushed shut very quickly, bolted fast, and barred. Gregor was startled by the sudden commotion behind him, so much so that his little limbs bent double under him. It was his sister who had been in such a hurry. She was already standing up, had waited, and then had sprung forward nimbly. Gregor had not heard anything of her approach. She cried out "Finally!" to her parents, as she turned the key in the lock.

"What now?" Gregor asked himself and looked around him in the darkness. He soon made the discovery that he could no longer move at all. He was not surprised at that. On the contrary, it struck him as unnatural that up to this point he had actually been able to move around with these thin little legs. Despite everything he felt relatively content. True, he had pains throughout his entire body, but it seemed to him that they were gradually becoming weaker and weaker and would finally go away completely. He hardly noticed the rotten apple in his back and the inflamed surrounding area, which were now entirely covered with soft dust. He remembered his family with deep feelings of love. In this whole business, his own conviction that he had to disappear was, if possible, even more firmly held than his sister's. He remained in this state of empty and peaceful reflection until the tower clock struck three in the morning. He lived long enough to see everything outside the window beginning to grow brighter. Then without his willing it, his head sank all the way down, and from his nostrils his last breath flowed weakly out.

Early in the morning the cleaning woman came. In her sheer

pt. ends p. 62

energy and haste she banged all the doors—in precisely the way people had already frequently asked her not to do—so much so that once she arrived a quiet sleep was no longer possible anywhere in the entire apartment. In her customary brief visit to Gregor she at first found nothing unusual. She thought he lay so immobile there on purpose and was playing the offended party. She gave him credit for as complete an understanding as possible. Since she happened to be holding the long broom in her hand, she tried to tickle Gregor with it from the door. When that was quite unsuccessful, she became irritated and poked Gregor a little, and only when she had shoved him from his place without any resistance did she take notice. When she realized the true state of affairs, her eyes grew large and she whistled to herself. However, she didn't restrain herself for long. She pulled open the door of the bedroom and yelled in a loud voice into the darkness, "Come and look. It's kicked the bucket. It's lying there. It's completely snuffed it!"

The Samsas sat upright in their double bed and had to get over their fright at the cleaning woman before they managed to grasp her message. But then Mr. and Mrs. Samsa climbed very quickly out of bed, one on either side. Mr. Samsa threw the bedspread over his shoulders, Mrs. Samsa came out only in her nightshirt, and like this they stepped into Gregor's room. Meanwhile, the door of the living room, where Grete had been sleeping since the lodgers had arrived on the scene, had also opened. She was fully clothed, as if she had not slept at all; her white face also seemed to indicate that.

"Dead?" said Mrs. Samsa and looked questioningly at the cleaning woman, although she could have checked everything on her own—and indeed it was all clear enough even without checking anything.

"I should say so," said the cleaning woman and, by way of proof, poked Gregor's body with the broom a considerable distance more to the side. Mrs. Samsa made a movement as if she wished to restrain the broom but did not do it.

"Well," said Mr. Samsa, "now we can give thanks to God." He crossed himself, and the three women followed his example. Grete, who did not take her eyes off the corpse, said, "Just look how thin he was. He has eaten nothing for such a long time. The meals which came in here came out again exactly the same." In fact, Gregor's body was completely flat and dry. That was apparent really for the first time, now that he was no longer raised on his small limbs and nothing else distracted one from looking.

"Grete, come and join us for a moment," said Mrs. Samsa with a melancholy smile, and Grete went, not without looking back at the corpse, following her parents into the bedroom. The cleaning woman shut the door and opened the window wide. In spite of the early morning, the fresh air was partly tinged with warmth. It was already almost the end of March.

The three lodgers stepped out of their room and looked around for their breakfast, astonished that they had been forgotten. The middle one of the gentlemen asked the cleaning woman grumpily, "Where is the breakfast?" However, she laid her finger to her lips and then quickly and silently indicated to the lodgers that they could come into Gregor's room. So they came and stood in the room, which was already quite bright, around Gregor's corpse, their hands in the pockets of their somewhat worn jackets.

Then the door of the bedroom opened, and Mr. Samsa appeared in his uniform, with his wife on one arm and his daughter on the other. All were a little tear stained. Now and then Grete pressed her face into her father's arm.

"Get out of my apartment immediately," said Mr. Samsa and pointed to the door, without letting go of the women.

"What do you mean?" said the middle lodger, somewhat dismayed and with a sugary smile. The two others kept their hands behind them and constantly rubbed them against each other, as if in joyful anticipation of a great squabble which must end up in their favor.

"I mean exactly what I say," replied Mr. Samsa, and, with his

pt. ends p. 62

two female companions, went directly up to the lodger. The latter at first stood there motionless and looked at the floor, as if matters were arranging themselves in a new way in his head.

"All right, then we'll go," he said and looked up at Mr. Samsa as if, suddenly overcome by humility, he was even asking fresh permission for this decision. Mr. Samsa merely nodded briefly and repeatedly to him with his eyes open wide. Following that, with long strides the lodger did actually go out into the hall. His two friends had already been listening for a while with their hands quite still, and now they hopped smartly after him, as if afraid that Mr. Samsa could step into the hall ahead of them and disturb their reunion with their leader. In the hall all three of them took their hats from the coat rack, pulled their canes from the umbrella stand, bowed silently, and left the apartment. In what turned out to be an entirely groundless mistrust, Mr. Samsa stepped with the two women out onto the landing, leaned against the railing, and looked over as the three lodgers slowly but steadily made their way down the long staircase, disappeared on each floor in a certain turn of the stairwell, and in a few seconds reappeared again. The further down they went, the more the Samsa family lost interest in them, and when a butcher's assistant with a tray on his head came up to meet them and then with a proud bearing ascended the stairs high above them, Mr. Samsa, together with the women, soon left the banister, and they all returned, as if relieved, back into their apartment.

They decided to pass that day resting and going for a stroll. Not only had they earned this break from work, but there was no question that they really needed it. And so they sat down at the table and wrote three letters of apology: Mr. Samsa to his supervisor, Mrs. Samsa to her client, and Grete to her proprietor. During the writing the cleaning woman came in to say that she was going off, for her morning work was finished. The three people writing at first merely nodded, without glancing up. Only when the cleaning woman was still unwilling to depart, did they look up annoyed. "Well?" asked Mr. Samsa. The cleaning woman stood smiling in the doorway, as if she had a great stroke of luck to report to the family but would only do it if she was questioned thoroughly. The almost upright small ostrich feather in her hat, which had irritated Mr. Samsa during her entire service with them, swayed lightly in all directions. "All right then, what do you really want?" asked Mrs. Samsa, whom the cleaning lady respected more than the others.

"Well," answered the cleaning woman, smiling so happily she couldn't go on speaking right away, "you mustn't worry about throwing out that rubbish from the next room. It's all taken care of."

Mrs. Samsa and Grete bent down to their letters, as though they wanted to go on writing. Mr. Samsa, who saw that the cleaning woman would now want to describe everything in detail, decisively prevented her with an outstretched hand. Since she was not allowed to explain, she remembered the great hurry she was in, and called out, clearly insulted, "Bye bye, everyone," then turned around furiously and left the apartment with a fearful slamming of the door.

"This evening she'll be given notice," said Mr. Samsa, but he got no answer from either his wife or from his daughter, because the cleaning woman seemed to have once again upset the tranquility they had just attained. The women got up, went to the window, and remained there, with their arms about each other. Mr. Samsa turned around in his chair in their direction and observed them quietly for a while. Then he called out, "All right, come here then. Let's set aside these old matters once and for all. And have a little consideration for me." The women attended to him at once. They rushed to him, caressed him, and quickly ended their letters.

Then all three left the apartment together, something they had not done for months now, and took the electric tram into the open air outside the city. The car in which they were sitting by themselves was wholly flooded by the warm sun. Leaning back comfortably in their seats, they talked to each other about future prospects, and they discovered that on closer observation

pt. ends next p.

these were not at all bad, for the three of them had not really questioned each other about their employment at all. Each of their positions was extremely favorable and offered especially promising future prospects. The greatest improvement in their situation at this point, of course, would have to come from a change of dwelling. They would now like to rent a smaller and cheaper apartment but better situated and generally more practical than the present one, which Gregor had chosen. While they amused themselves chatting in this way, it struck Mr. and Mrs. Samsa, almost at the same moment, as they looked at their daughter, who was getting more animated all the time, how she had blossomed recently, in spite of all the troubles which had made her cheeks pale, into a beautiful and voluptuous young woman. Growing more silent and almost unconsciously understanding each other in their glances, they thought that the time was now at hand to seek out a good honest man for her. And it was something of a confirmation of their new dreams and good intentions when at the end of their journey their daughter stood up first and stretched her young body.

& SOME OTHER STORIES.

AN IMPERIAL MESSAGE

The Emperor—so they say—has sent a message, directly from his death bed, to you alone, his pathetic subject, a tiny shadow which has taken refuge at the furthest distance from the imperial sun. He ordered the herald to kneel down beside his bed and whispered the message in his ear. He thought it was so important that he had the herald speak it back to him. He confirmed the accuracy of verbal message by nodding his head. And in front of the entire crowd of those witnessing his death—all the obstructing walls have been broken down, and all the great ones of his empire are standing in a circle on the broad and high soaring flights of stairs—in front of all of them he dispatched his herald. The messenger started off at once, a powerful, tireless man. Sticking one arm out and then another, he makes his way through the crowd. If he runs into resistance, he points to his breast where there is a sign of the sun. So he moves forward easily, unlike anyone else. But the crowd is so huge; its dwelling places are infinite. If there were an open field, how he would fly along, and soon you would hear the marvelous pounding of his fist on your door. But instead of that, how futile are all his efforts. He is still forcing his way through the private rooms of the innermost palace. Never will he win his way through. And if he did manage that, nothing would have been achieved. He would have to fight his way down the steps, and, if he managed to do that, nothing would have been achieved. He would have to stride through the courtyards, and after the courtyards through the second palace encircling the first, and, then again, through stairs and courtyards, and then, once again, a palace, and so on for thousands of years. And if he finally burst through the outermost door—but that can never, never happen—the royal capital city, the center of the world, is still there in front of him, piled high and full of sediment. No one pushes his way through here, certainly not someone with a message from a dead man. But you sit at your window and dream of that message when evening comes.

THE HUNTER GRACCHUS

Two boys were sitting on the wall by the jetty[1] playing dice. A man was reading a newspaper on the steps of a monument in the shadow of a hero wielding a saber. A young girl was filling her tub with water at a fountain. A fruit seller was lying close to his produce and looking out to sea. Through the empty openings of the door and window of a bar two men could be seen drinking wine in the back. The landlord was sitting at a table in the front dozing. A small boat glided lightly into the small harbor, as if it were being carried over the water. A man in a blue jacket climbed out onto land and pulled the ropes through the rings. Behind the man from the boat, two other men in dark coats with silver buttons carried a bier,[2] on which, under a large silk scarf with a floral pattern and fringe, a man was obviously lying.

No one bothered with the newcomers on the jetty, even when they set the bier down to wait for their helmsman,[3] who was still working with the ropes. No one came up to them, no one asked them any questions, no one took a closer look at them.

The helmsman was further held up a little by a woman with disheveled hair, who now appeared on deck with a child at her breast. Then he came on, pointing to a yellowish two-story

---

[1] A pier or dock.

[2] A carriage or framework for conveying corpses to the grave.

[3] One who steers a boat or ship.

house which rose close by, directly on the left near the water. The bearers took up their load and carried it through the low door furnished with slender columns. A small boy opened a window, noticed immediately how the group was disappearing into the house, and quickly shut the window again. The door closed. It had been fashioned with care out of black oak wood. A flock of doves, which up to this point had been flying around the bell tower, came down in front of the house. The doves gathered before the door, as if their food was stored inside the house. One flew right up to the first floor and pecked at the window pane. They were brightly colored, well cared for, lively animals. With a large sweep of her hand the woman on the boat threw some seeds toward them. They ate them up and then flew over to the woman.

A man in a top hat with a mourning ribbon came down one of the small, narrow, steeply descending lanes which led to the harbor. He looked around him attentively. Everything upset him. He winced at the sight of some garbage in a corner. There were fruit peels on the steps of the monument. As he went by, he pushed them off with his cane. He knocked on the door of the house, while at the same time taking off his top hat with his black-gloved right hand. It was opened immediately, and about fifty small boys, lined up in two rows in a long corridor, bowed to him.

The helmsman came down the stairs, met the gentleman, and led him upstairs. On the first floor he accompanied him around the slight, delicately built balcony surrounding the courtyard, and, as the boys crowded behind them at a respectful distance, both men stepped into a large cool room at the back. From it one could not see a facing house, only a bare gray-black rock wall. Those who had carried the bier were busy setting up and lighting some long candles at its head. But these provided no light. They only made the previously still shadows jump and flicker across the walls. The shawl was pulled back off the bier. On it lay a man with wildly unkempt hair and beard and a brown skin—he looked rather like a hunter. He lay there motionless, apparently without breathing, his eyes closed, although his surroundings were the only thing indicating that it could be a corpse.

The gentleman stepped over to the bier, laid a hand on the forehead of the man lying there, then knelt down and prayed. The helmsman gave a sign to the bearers to leave the room. They went out, drove away the boys who had gathered outside, and shut the door. The gentleman, however, was apparently still not satisfied with this stillness. He looked at the helmsman. The latter understood and went through a side door into the next room. The man on the bier immediately opened his eyes, turned his face with a painful smile toward the gentleman, and said, "Who are you?" Without any surprise, the gentleman got up from his kneeling position and answered, "The burgomaster[4] of Riva."

The man on the bier nodded, pointed to a chair by stretching his arm out feebly, and then, after the burgomaster had accepted his invitation, said, "Yes, I knew that, Burgomaster, but when I first glance around I've always forgotten it all—everything is going in circles around me, and it's better for me to ask, even when I know everything. You also presumably know that I am the hunter Gracchus."

"Of course," said the burgomaster. "I received the news today, during the night. We had been sleeping for some time. Then around midnight my wife called, 'Salvatore'—that's my name—'look at the dove in the window!' It was really a dove, but as large as a rooster. It flew up to my ear and said, 'Tomorrow the dead hunter Gracchus is coming. Welcome him in the name of the city.'"

The hunter nodded and pushed the tip of his tongue between his lips. "Yes, the doves fly here before me. But do you believe, Burgomaster, that I am to remain in Riva?"

"That I cannot yet say," answered the burgomaster. "Are you dead?"

"Yes," said the hunter, "as you see. Many years ago—it must

[4] The principal magistrate, comparable to a mayor, of a Dutch, Flemish, German, Austrian, or Swiss city or town.

story ends p. 74

have been a great many years ago—I fell from a rock in the Black Forest—that's in Germany—as I was tracking a chamois.[5] Since then I've been dead."

"But you're also alive," said the burgomaster.

"To a certain extent," said the hunter, "to a certain extent I am also alive. My death ship lost its way—a wrong turn of the helm, a moment when the helmsman was not paying attention, a distraction from my wonderful homeland—I don't know what it was. I only know that I remain on the earth and that since that time my ship has journeyed over earthly waters. So I—who only wanted to live in my own mountains—travel on after my death through all the countries of the earth."

"And have you no share in the world beyond?" asked the burgomaster wrinkling his brow.

The hunter answered, "I am always on the immense staircase leading up to it. I roam around on this infinitely wide flight of steps, sometimes up, sometimes down, sometimes to the right, sometimes to the left, always in motion. From being a hunter I've become a butterfly. Don't laugh."

"I'm not laughing," answered the burgomaster.

"That's very considerate of you," said the hunter. "I am always moving. But when I go through the greatest upward motion and the door is shining right above me, I wake up on my old ship, still drearily stranded in some earthly stretch of water. The basic mistake of my earlier death grins at me in my cabin. Julia, the wife of the helmsman, knocks and brings to me on the bier the morning drink of the country whose coast we are sailing by at the time. I lie on a wooden plank bed, wearing—I'm no delight to look at—a filthy shroud, my hair and beard, black and gray, are inextricably intertangled, my legs covered by a large silk women's scarf, with a floral pattern and long fringes. At my head stands a church candle which illuminates me. On the wall opposite me is a small picture, evidently of a bushman aiming his spear at me

---

[5] A sure-footed goat antelope inhabiting mountains of Europe and southwest Asia.

and concealing himself as much as possible behind a splendidly painted shield. On board ship one comes across many stupid pictures, but this is one of the stupidest. Beyond that my wooden cage is completely empty. Through a hole in the side wall the warm air of the southern nights comes in, and I hear the water lapping against the old boat.

I have been lying here since the time when I—the still living hunter Gracchus—was pursuing a chamois to its home in the Black Forest and fell. Everything took place as it should. I followed, fell down, bled to death in a ravine, was dead, and this boat was supposed to carry me to the other side. I still remember how happily I stretched myself out here on the planking for the first time. The mountains have never heard me singing the way these four still shadowy walls did then.

I had been happy to be alive and was happy to be dead. Before I came on board, I gladly threw away my rag-tag collection of guns and bags, even the hunting rifle which I had always carried so proudly, and slipped into the shroud like a young girl into her wedding dress. There I lay down and waited. Then the accident happened."

"A nasty fate," said the burgomaster, raising his hand in a gesture of depreciation,[6] "and you are not to blame for it in any way?"

"No," said the hunter. "I was a hunter. Is there any blame in that? I was raised to be a hunter in the Black Forest, where at that time there were still wolves. I lay in wait, shot, hit the target, removed the skin—is there any blame in that? My work was blessed. 'The great hunter of the Black Forest'—that's what they called me. Is that something bad?"

"It not up to me to decide that," said the burgomaster, "but it seems to me as well that there's no blame there. But then who is to blame?"

"The boatman," said the hunter. "No one will read what I write

---

[6] Disparagement.

here, no one will come to help me. If people were assigned the task of helping me, all the doors of all the houses would remain closed, all the windows would be shut, they would all lie in bed, with sheets thrown over their heads, the entire earth would be a hostel for the night. And that makes good sense, for no one knows of me, and if he did, he would have no idea of where I was staying, and if he knew that, he would still not know how to keep me there, and so he would not know how to help me. The thought of wanting to help me is a sickness and has to be cured with bed rest.

"I know that, and so I do not cry out to summon help, even if at moments when I have no self-control, for example right now, I do think about that very seriously. But to get rid of such ideas I need only look around and recall where I am and where—and this I can assert with full confidence—I have lived for centuries.

"That's extraordinary," said the burgomaster, "extraordinary. And now are you intending to remain with us in Riva?"

"I have no intentions," said the hunter with a smile and, to make up for his mocking tone, laid a hand on the burgomaster's knee. "I am here. I don't know any more than that. There's nothing more I can do. My boat is without a helm—it journeys with the wind which blows in the deepest regions of death."

A HUNGER ARTIST

In the last decades interest in hunger artists has declined considerably. Whereas in earlier days there was good money to be earned putting on major productions of this sort under one's own management, nowadays that is totally impossible. Those were different times. Back then the hunger artist captured the attention of the entire city. From day to day while the fasting lasted, participation increased. Everyone wanted to see the hunger artist at least daily. During the final days there were people with subscription tickets who sat all day in front of the small barred cage. And there were even viewing hours at night, their impact heightened by torchlight. On fine days the cage was dragged out into the open air, and then the hunger artist was put on display particularly for the children. While for grown-ups the hunger artist was often merely a joke, something they participated in because it was fashionable, the children looked on amazed, their mouths open, holding each other's hands for safety, as he sat there on scattered straw—spurning a chair—in black tights, looking pale, with his ribs sticking out prominently, sometimes nodding politely, answering questions with a forced smile, even sticking his arm out through the bars to let people feel how emaciated he was, but then completely sinking back into himself, so that he paid no attention to anything, not even to what was so important to him, the striking of the clock, which was the single furnishing in the cage, merely looking out in front of him with his eyes almost shut and now and then sipping from a tiny glass of water to moisten his lips.

Apart from the changing groups of spectators there were also constant observers chosen by the public—strangely enough they were usually butchers—who, always three at a time, were given the task of observing the hunger artist day and night, so that he didn't get something to eat in some secret manner. It was, however, merely a formality, introduced to reassure the masses, for those who understood knew well enough that during the period of fasting the hunger artist would never, under any circumstances, have eaten the slightest thing, not even if compelled by force. The honor of his art forbade it. Naturally, none of the watchers understood that. Sometimes there were nightly groups of watchers who carried out their vigil very laxly, deliberately sitting together in a distant corner and putting all their attention into playing cards there, clearly intending to allow the hunger artist a small refreshment, which, according to their way of thinking, he could get from some secret supplies. Nothing was more excruciating to the hunger artist than such watchers. They depressed him. They made his fasting terribly difficult. Sometimes he overcame his weakness and sang during the time they were observing, for as long as he could keep it up, to show people how unjust their suspicions about him were. But that was little help. For then they just wondered among themselves about his skill at being able to eat even while singing. He much preferred the observers who sat down right against the bars and, not satisfied with the dim backlighting of the room, illuminated him with electric flashlights. The glaring light didn't bother him in the slightest. Generally he couldn't sleep at all, and he could always doze under any lighting and at any hour, even in an overcrowded, noisy auditorium. With such observers, he was very happily prepared to spend the entire night without sleeping. He was very pleased to joke with them, to recount stories from his nomadic life and then, in turn, to listen to their stories—doing everything just to keep them awake, so that he could keep showing them once again that he had nothing to eat in his cage and that he was fasting as none of them could.

He was happiest, however, when morning came and a lavish breakfast was brought for them at his own expense, on which they hurled themselves with the appetite of healthy men after a hard night's work without sleep. True, there were still people who wanted to see in this breakfast an unfair means of influencing the observers, but that was going too far, and if they were asked whether they wanted to undertake the observers' night shift for its own sake, without the breakfast, they excused themselves. But nonetheless they stood by their suspicions.

However, it was, in general, part of fasting that these doubts were inextricably associated with it. For, in fact, no one was in a position to spend time watching the hunger artist every day and night, so no one could know, on the basis of his own observation, whether this was a case of truly uninterrupted, flawless fasting. The hunger artist himself was the only one who could know that and, at the same time, the only spectator capable of being completely satisfied with his own fasting. But the reason he was never satisfied was something different. Perhaps it was not fasting at all which made him so very emaciated that many people, to their own regret, had to stay away from his performance, because they couldn't bear to look at him. For he was also so skeletal out of dissatisfaction with himself, because he alone knew something that even initiates didn't know—how easy it was to fast. It was the easiest thing in the world. About this he did not remain silent, but people did not believe him. At best they thought he was being modest. Most of them, however, believed he was a publicity seeker or a total swindler, for whom, at all events, fasting was easy, because he understood how to make it easy, and then had the nerve to half admit it. He had to accept all that. Over the years he had become accustomed to it. But this dissatisfaction kept gnawing at his insides all the time and never yet—and this one had to say to his credit—had he left the cage of his own free will after any period of fasting.

story ends p. 86

The impresario[1] had set the maximum length of time for the fast at forty days—he would never allow the fasting go on beyond that point, not even in the cosmopolitan cities. And, in fact, he had a good reason. Experience had shown that for about forty days one could increasingly whip up a city's interest by gradually increasing advertising, but that then the people turned away—one could demonstrate a significant decline in popularity. In this respect, there were, of course, small differences among different towns and among different countries, but as a rule it was true that forty days was the maximum length of time.

So then on the fortieth day the door of the cage—which was covered with flowers—was opened, an enthusiastic audience filled the amphitheater, a military band played, two doctors entered the cage, in order to take the necessary measurements of the hunger artist, the results were announced to the auditorium through a megaphone, and finally two young ladies arrived, happy about the fact that they were the ones who had just been selected by lot, seeking to lead the hunger artist down a couple of steps out of the cage, where on a small table a carefully chosen hospital meal was laid out. And at this moment the hunger artist always fought back. Of course, he still freely laid his bony arms in the helpful outstretched hands of the ladies bending over him, but he did not want to stand up. Why stop right now after forty days? He could have kept going for even longer, for an unlimited length of time. Why stop right now, when he was in his best form, indeed, not yet even in his best fasting form? Why did people want to rob him of the fame of fasting longer, not just so that he could become the greatest hunger artist of all time, which he probably was already, but also so that he could surpass himself in some unimaginable way, for he felt there were no limits to his capacity for fasting. Why did this crowd, which pretended to admire him so much, have so little patience with him? If he kept going and kept fasting longer, why would they not tolerate it?

[1] A manager or producer of entertainment.

Then, too, he was tired and felt good sitting in the straw. Now he was supposed to stand up straight and tall and go to eat, something which, when he just imagined it, made him feel nauseous right away. With great difficulty he repressed mentioning this only out of consideration for the women. And he looked up into the eyes of these women, apparently so friendly but in reality so cruel, and shook his excessively heavy head on his feeble neck.

But then happened what always happened. The impresario came and in silence—the music made talking impossible—raised his arms over the hunger artist, as if inviting heaven to look upon its work here on the straw, this unfortunate martyr, something the hunger artist certainly was, only in a completely different sense, then grabbed the hunger artist around his thin waist, in the process wanting with his exaggerated caution to make people believe that here he had to deal with something fragile, and handed him over—not without secretly shaking him a little, so that the hunger artist's legs and upper body swung back and forth uncontrollably—to the women, who had in the meantime turned as pale as death. At this point, the hunger artist endured everything. His head lay on his chest—it was as if it had inexplicably rolled around and just stopped there—his body was arched back, his legs, in an impulse of self-preservation, pressed themselves together at the knees, but scraped the ground, as if they were not really on the floor but were looking for the real ground, and the entire weight of his body, admittedly very small, lay against one of the women, who appealed for help with flustered breath, for she had not imagined her post of honor would be like this, and then stretched her neck as far as possible, to keep her face from the least contact with the hunger artist, but then, when she couldn't manage this and her more fortunate companion didn't come to her assistance but trembled and remained content to hold in front of her the hunger artist's hand, that small bundle of knuckles, she broke into tears, to the delighted laughter of the auditorium, and had to be relieved by an attendant who had been standing ready for some time. Then came the meal.

story ends p. 86

The impresario put a little food into the mouth of the hunger artist, now half unconscious, as if fainting, and kept up a cheerful patter designed to divert attention away from the hunger artist's condition. Then a toast was proposed to the public, which was supposedly whispered to the impresario by the hunger artist, the orchestra confirmed everything with a great fanfare, people dispersed, and no one had the right to be dissatisfied with the event, no one except the hunger artist—he was always the only one.

He lived this way, taking small regular breaks, for many years, apparently in the spotlight, honored by the world, but for all that his mood was usually gloomy, and it kept growing gloomier all the time, because no one understood how to take him seriously. But how was he to find consolation? What was there left for him to wish for? And if a good-natured man who felt sorry for him ever wanted to explain to him that his sadness probably came from his fasting, then it could happen that the hunger artist responded with an outburst of rage and began to shake the bars like an animal, frightening everyone. But the impresario had a way of punishing moments like this, something he was happy to use. He would make an apology for the hunger artist to the assembled public, conceding that the irritability had been provoked only by his fasting, something quite intelligible to well-fed people and capable of excusing the behavior of the hunger artist without further explanation. From there he would move on to speak about the equally hard to understand claim of the hunger artist that he could go on fasting for much longer than he was doing. He would praise the lofty striving, the good will, and the great self-denial no doubt contained in this claim, but then would try to contradict it simply by producing photographs, which were also on sale, for in the pictures one could see the hunger artist on the fortieth day of his fast, in bed, almost dead from exhaustion. Although the hunger artist was very familiar with this perversion of the truth, it always strained his nerves again and was too much for him. What was a result of the premature ending of the fast people were now proposing as its cause! It was impossible to fight against this lack of understanding, against this world of misunderstanding. In good faith he always listened eagerly to the impresario at the bars of his cage, but each time, once the photographs came out, he would let go of the bars and, with a sigh, sink back into the straw, and a reassured public could come up again and view him.

When those who had witnessed such scenes thought back on them a few years later, often they were unable to understand themselves. For in the meantime that change mentioned above had set it. It happened almost immediately. There may have been more profound reasons for it, but who bothered to discover what they were? At any rate, one day the pampered hunger artist saw himself abandoned by the crowd of pleasure seekers, who preferred to stream to other attractions. The impresario chased around half of Europe one more time with him, to see whether he could still re-discover the old interest here and there. It was all futile. It was as if a secret agreement against the fasting performances had developed everywhere. Naturally, it couldn't really have happened all at once, and people later remembered some things which in the days of intoxicating success they hadn't paid sufficient attention to, some inadequately suppressed indications, but now it was too late to do anything to counter them. Of course, it was certain that the popularity of fasting would return once more someday, but for those now alive that was no consolation. What was the hunger artist to do now? A man whom thousands of people had cheered on could not display himself in show booths at small fun fairs. The hunger artist was not only too old to take up a different profession, but was fanatically devoted to fasting more than anything else. So he said farewell to the impresario, an incomparable companion on his life's road, and let himself be hired by a large circus. In order to spare his own feelings, he didn't even look at the terms of his contract at all.

A large circus with its huge number of men, animals, and gimmicks, which are constantly being let go and replenished, can

story ends p. 86

use anyone at any time, even a hunger artist, provided, of course, his demands are modest. Moreover, in this particular case it was not only the hunger artist himself who was engaged, but also his old and famous name. In fact, given the characteristic nature of his art, which was not diminished by his advancing age, one could never claim that a worn out artist, who no longer stood at the pinnacle of his ability, wanted to escape to a quiet position in the circus. On the contrary, the hunger artist declared that he could fast just as well as in earlier times—something that was entirely credible. Indeed, he even affirmed that if people would let him do what he wanted—and he was promised this without further ado—he would really now legitimately amaze the world for the first time, an assertion which, however, given the mood of the time, which the hunger artist in his enthusiasm easily overlooked, only brought smiles from the experts.

However, basically the hunger artist had not forgotten his sense of the way things really were, and he took it as self-evident that people would not set him and his cage up as the star attraction somewhere in the middle of the arena, but would move him outside in some other readily accessible spot near the animal stalls. Huge brightly painted signs surrounded the cage and announced what there was to look at there. During the intervals in the main performance, when the general public pushed out toward the menagerie in order to see the animals, they could hardly avoid moving past the hunger artist and stopping there a moment. They would perhaps have remained with him longer, if those pushing up behind them in the narrow passageway, who did not understand this pause on the way to the animal stalls they wanted to see, had not made a longer peaceful observation impossible. This was also the reason why the hunger artist began to tremble at these visiting hours, which he naturally used to long for as the main purpose of his life. In the early days he could hardly wait for the pauses in the performances. He had looked forward with delight to the crowd pouring around him, until he became convinced only too quickly—and even the most stubborn, almost deliberate self-deception could not hold out against the experience—that, judging by their intentions, most of these people were, again and again without exception, only visiting the menagerie.[2] And this view from a distance still remained his most beautiful moment. For when they had come right up to him, he immediately got an earful from the shouting of the two steadily increasing groups, the ones who wanted to take their time looking at the hunger artist, not with any understanding but on a whim or from mere defiance—for him these ones were soon the more painful—and a second group of people whose only demand was to go straight to the animal stalls.

Once the large crowds had passed, the late comers would arrive, and although there was nothing preventing these people anymore from sticking around for as long as they wanted, they rushed past with long strides, almost without a sideways glance, to get to the animals in time. And it was an all-too-rare stroke of luck when the father of a family came by with his children, pointed his finger at the hunger artist, gave a detailed explanation about what was going on here, and talked of earlier years, when he had been present at similar but incomparably more magnificent performances, and then the children, because they had been inadequately prepared at school and in life, always stood around still uncomprehendingly. What was fasting to them? But nonetheless the brightness of the look in their searching eyes revealed something of new and more gracious times coming. Perhaps, the hunger artist said to himself sometimes, everything would be a little better if his location were not quite so near the animal stalls. That way it would be easy for people to make their choice, to say nothing of the fact that he was very upset and constantly depressed by the stink from the stalls, the animals' commotion at night, the pieces of raw meat dragged past him for the carnivorous beasts, and the roars at feeding time. But he did not dare to approach the administration about it. In any case, he

---

[2] An assortment or collection of live wild animals kept in captivity for exhibition.

story ends p. 86

had the animals to thank for the crowds of visitors among whom, here and there, there could be one destined for him. And who knew where they would hide him if he wished to remind them of his existence and, along with that, of the fact that, strictly speaking, he was only an obstacle on the way to the menagerie.

A small obstacle, at any rate, a constantly diminishing obstacle. People got used to the strange notion that in these times they would want to pay attention to a hunger artist, and with this habitual awareness the judgment on him was pronounced. He might fast as well as he could—and he did—but nothing could save him anymore. People went straight past him. Try to explain the art of fasting to anyone! If someone doesn't feel it, then he cannot be made to understand it. The beautiful signs became dirty and illegible. People tore them down, and no one thought of replacing them. The small table with the number of days the fasting had lasted, which early on had been carefully renewed every day, remained unchanged for a long time, for after the first weeks the staff grew tired of even this small task. And so the hunger artist kept fasting on and on, as he once had dreamed about in earlier times, and he had no difficulty succeeding in achieving what he had predicted back then, but no one was counting the days—no one, not even the hunger artist himself, knew how great his achievement was by this point, and his heart grew heavy. And when once in a while a person strolling past stood there making fun of the old number and talking of a swindle, that was in a sense the stupidest lie which indifference and innate maliciousness could invent, for the hunger artist was not being deceptive—he was working honestly—but the world was cheating him of his reward.

Many days went by once more, and this, too, came to an end. Finally the cage caught the attention of a supervisor, and he asked the attendant why they had left this perfectly useful cage standing here unused with rotting straw inside. Nobody knew, until one man, with the help of the table with the number on it, remembered the hunger artist. They pushed the straw around with a pole and found the hunger artist in there.

"Are you still fasting?" the supervisor asked. "When are you finally going to stop?"

"Forgive me everything," whispered the hunger artist. Only the supervisor, who was pressing his ear up against the cage, understood him.

"Certainly," said the supervisor, tapping his forehead with his finger in order to indicate to the spectators the state the hunger artist was in, "we forgive you."

"I always wanted you to admire my fasting," said the hunger artist.

"But we do admire it," said the supervisor obligingly.

"But you shouldn't admire it," said the hunger artist.

"Well then, we don't admire it," said the supervisor, "but why shouldn't we admire it?"

"Because I had to fast. I can't do anything else," said the hunger artist.

"Just look at you," said the supervisor, "why can't you do anything else?"

"Because," said the hunger artist, lifting his head a little and, with his lips pursed as if for a kiss, speaking right into the supervisor's ear so that he wouldn't miss anything, "because I couldn't find a food which I enjoyed. If I had found that, believe me, I would not have made a spectacle of myself and would have eaten to my heart's content, like you and everyone else." Those were his last words, but in his failing eyes there was the firm, if no longer proud, conviction that he was continuing to fast.

"All right, tidy this up now," said the supervisor. And they buried the hunger artist along with the straw. But in his cage they put a young panther. Even for a person with the dullest mind it was clearly refreshing to see this wild animal throwing itself around in this cage, which had been dreary for such a long time. It lacked nothing. Without thinking about it for any length of time, the guards brought the animal food. It enjoyed the taste

story ends next p.

and never seemed to miss its freedom. This noble body, equipped with everything necessary, almost to the point of bursting, also appeared to carry freedom around with it. That seem to be located somewhere or other in its teeth, and its joy in living came with such strong passion from its throat that it was not easy for spectators to keep watching. But they controlled themselves, kept pressing around the cage, and had no desire to move on.

BEFORE THE LAW

Before the law sits a gatekeeper. To this gatekeeper comes a man from the country who asks to gain entry into the law. But the gatekeeper says that he cannot grant him entry at the moment. The man thinks about it and then asks if he will be allowed to come in later on. "It is possible," says the gatekeeper, "but not now." At the moment the gate to the law stands open, as always, and the gatekeeper walks to the side, so the man bends over in order to see through the gate into the inside. When the gate-keeper notices that, he laughs and says: "If it tempts you so much, try it in spite of my prohibition. But take note: I am powerful. And I am only the most lowly gatekeeper. But from room to room stand gatekeepers, each more powerful than the other. I can't endure even one glimpse of the third." The man from the country has not expected such difficulties: the law should always be accessible for everyone, he thinks, but as he now looks more closely at the gatekeeper in his fur coat, at his large pointed nose and his long, thin, black Tartar's beard, he decides that it would be better to wait until he gets permission to go inside. The gatekeeper gives him a stool and allows him to sit down at the side in front of the gate. There he sits for days and years. He makes many attempts to be let in, and he wears the gatekeeper out with his requests. The gatekeeper often interrogates him briefly, questioning him about his homeland and many other things, but they are indifferent questions, the kind great men put, and at the end he always tells him once more that he cannot let him inside yet. The man, who has equipped himself with many things for his journey, spends everything, no matter how valuable, to win over the gatekeeper. The latter takes it all but, as he does so, says, "I am taking this only so that you do not think you have failed to do anything." During the many years the man observes the gatekeeper almost continuously. He forgets the other gatekeepers, and this one seems to him the only obstacle for entry into the law. He curses the unlucky circumstance, in the first years thoughtlessly and out loud, later, as he grows old, he still mumbles to himself. He becomes childish and, since in the long years studying the gatekeeper he has come to know the fleas in his fur collar, he even asks the fleas to help him persuade the gatekeeper. Finally his eyesight grows weak, and he does not know whether things are really darker around him or whether his eyes are merely deceiving him. But he recognizes now in the darkness an illumination which breaks inextinguishably out of the gateway to the law. Now he no longer has much time to live. Before his death he gathers in his head all his experiences of the entire time up into one question which he has not yet put to the gatekeeper. He waves to him, since he can no longer lift up his stiffening body. The gatekeeper has to bend way down to him, for the great difference has changed things to the disadvantage of the man. "What do you still want to know, then?" asks the gatekeeper. "You are insatiable."

"Everyone strives after the law," says the man, "so how is that in these many years no one except me has requested entry?"

The gatekeeper sees that the man is already dying and, in order to reach his diminishing sense of hearing, he shouts at him, "Here no one else can gain entry, since this entrance was assigned only to you. I'm going now to close it."

IN THE PENAL COLONY

"It's a peculiar apparatus," said the Officer to the Traveler, gazing with a certain admiration at the device, with which he was, of course, thoroughly familiar. It appeared that the Traveler had responded to the invitation of the Commandant only out of politeness, when he had been invited to attend the execution of a soldier condemned for disobeying and insulting his superior. Of course, interest in the execution was not very high, not even in the penal colony itself. At least, here in the small, deep, sandy valley, closed in on all sides by barren slopes, apart from the Officer and the Traveler there were present only the Condemned, a vacant-looking man with a broad mouth and dilapidated hair and face, and the Soldier, who held the heavy chain to which were connected the small chains which bound the Condemned Man by his feet and wrist bones, as well as by his neck, and which were also linked to each other by connecting chains. The Condemned Man had an expression of such dog-like resignation that it looked as if one could set him free to roam around the slopes and would only have to whistle at the start of the execution for him to return.

The Traveler had little interest in the apparatus and walked back and forth behind the Condemned Man, almost visibly indifferent, while the Officer took care of the final preparations. Sometimes he crawled under the apparatus, which was built deep into the earth, and sometimes he climbed up a ladder to inspect the upper parts. These were really jobs which could have been left to a mechanic, but the Officer carried them out with great enthusiasm, maybe because he was particularly fond of this apparatus or maybe because there was some other reason why one could not trust the work to anyone else. "It's all ready now!" he finally cried and climbed back down the ladder. He was unusually tired, breathing with his mouth wide open, and he had pushed two fine lady's handkerchiefs under the collar of his uniform.

"These uniforms are really too heavy for the tropics," the Traveler said, instead of asking some questions about the apparatus, as the Officer had expected.

"That's true," said the Officer. He washed the oil and grease from his dirty hands in a bucket of water standing ready, "but they mean home, and we don't want to lose our homeland."

"Now, have a look at this apparatus," he added immediately, drying his hands with a towel and pointing to the device. "Up to this point I had to do some work by hand, but from now on the apparatus should work entirely on its own."

The Traveler nodded and followed the Officer. The latter tried to protect himself against all eventualities by saying, "Of course, breakdowns do happen. I really hope none will occur today, but we must be prepared for it. The apparatus is supposed to keep going for twelve hours without interruption. But if any breakdowns do occur, they'll only be very minor, and we'll deal with them right away."

"Don't you want to sit down?" he asked finally, as he pulled out a chair from a pile of cane chairs and offered it to the Traveler. The latter could not refuse. He sat on the edge of the pit, into which he cast a fleeting glance. It was not very deep. On one side of the hole the piled earth was heaped up into a wall; on the other side stood the apparatus. "I don't know," the officer said, "whether the Commandant has already explained the apparatus to you." The Traveler made a vague gesture with his hand. That was good enough for the Officer, for now he could explain the apparatus himself.

"This apparatus," he said, grasping a connecting rod and leaning against it, "is our previous Commandant's invention. I also worked with him on the very first tests and took part in all the work right up to its completion. However, the credit for the invention belongs to him alone. Have you heard of our previous Commandant? No? Well, I'm not claiming too much when I say that the organization of the entire penal colony is his work. We, his friends, already knew at the time of his death that the administration of the colony was so self-contained that even if his successor had a thousand new plans in mind, he would not be able to alter anything of the old plan, at least not for several years. And our prediction has held. The New Commandant has had to recognize that. It's a shame that you didn't know the previous Commandant!"

"However," the Officer said, interrupting himself, "I'm chattering, and his apparatus stands here in front of us. As you see, it consists of three parts. With the passage of time certain popular names have been developed for each of these parts. The one underneath is called the bed, the upper one is called the inscriber, and here in the middle, this moving part is called the harrow."[1]

"The harrow?" the Traveler asked. He had not been listening with full attention. The sun was excessively strong, trapped in the shadowless valley, and one could hardly collect one's thoughts. So the Officer appeared to him all the more admirable in his tight tunic weighed down with epaulettes[2] and festooned[3] with braid, ready to go on parade, as he explained the matter so eagerly and, while he was talking, adjusted screws here and there with a screwdriver.

The Soldier appeared to be in a state similar to the Traveler.

[1] An agricultural implement with spikelike teeth, tines, or discs set within a heavy frame which is dragged over plowed land to level ground and break up clods.

[2] Ornamental shoulder pieces on an item of clothing, typically on the coat or jacket of a military uniform.

[3] Adorned; decorated.

story ends p. 120

He had wound the Condemned Man's chain around both his wrists and was supporting himself with his hand on his weapon, letting his head hang backward, not bothering about anything. The Traveler was not surprised at that, for the Officer spoke French, and clearly neither the Soldier nor the Condemned Man understood the language. So it was all the more striking that the Condemned Man, in spite of that, did what he could to follow the Officer's explanation. With a sort of sleepy persistence he kept directing his gaze to the place where the Officer had just pointed, and when the question from the Traveler interrupted the Officer, the Condemned Man looked at the Traveler, too, just as the Officer was doing.

"Yes, the harrow," said the Officer. "The name fits. The needles are arranged as in a harrow, and the whole thing is driven like a harrow, although it stays in one place and is, in principle, much more artistic. You'll understand in a moment. The condemned is laid out here on the bed. First, I'll describe the apparatus and only then let the procedure go to work. That way you'll be able to follow it better. Also a sprocket in the inscriber is excessively worn. It really squeaks. When it's in motion one can hardly make oneself understood. Unfortunately replacement parts are difficult to come by in this place. So, here is the bed, as I said. The whole thing is completely covered with a layer of cotton wool, the purpose of which you'll find out in a moment. The condemned man is laid out on his stomach on the cotton wool—naked, of course. There are straps for the hands here, for the feet here, and for the throat here, to tie him in securely. At the head of the bed here, where the man, as I have mentioned, first lies face down, is this small protruding lump of felt, which can easily be adjusted so that it presses right into the man's mouth. Its purpose is to prevent him screaming and biting his tongue to pieces. Of course, the man has to let the felt in his mouth—otherwise the straps around his throat would break his neck."

"That's cotton wool?" asked the Traveler and bent down.

"Yes, it is," said the Officer smiling, "feel it for yourself."

He took the Traveler's hand and led him over to the bed. "It's a specially prepared cotton wool. That's why it looks so unrecognizable. I'll get around to mentioning its purpose in a moment." The Traveler was already being won over a little to the apparatus. With his hand over his eyes to protect them from the sun, he looked at the apparatus in the hole. It was a massive construction. The bed and the inscriber were the same size and looked like two dark chests. The inscriber was set about two meters above the bed, and the two were joined together at the corners by four brass rods, which almost reflected the sun. The harrow hung between the chests on a band of steel.

The Officer had hardly noticed the earlier indifference of the Traveler, but he did have a sense now of how the latter's interest was being aroused for the first time. So he paused in his explanation in order to allow the Traveler time to observe the apparatus undisturbed. The Condemned Man imitated the Traveler, but since he could not put his hand over his eyes, he blinked upward with his eyes uncovered.

"So now the man is lying down," said the Traveler. He leaned back in his chair and crossed his legs.

"Yes," said the Officer, pushing his cap back a little and running his hand over his hot face. "Now, listen. Both the bed and the inscriber have their own electric batteries. The bed needs them for itself, and the inscriber for the harrow. As soon as the man is strapped in securely, the bed is set in motion. It quivers with tiny, very rapid oscillations from side to side and up and down simultaneously. You will have seen similar devices in mental hospitals. Only with our bed all movements are precisely calibrated, for they must be meticulously coordinated with the movements of the harrow. But it's the harrow which has the job of actually carrying out the sentence."

"What is the sentence?" the Traveler asked.

"You don't even know that?" asked the Officer in astonishment and bit his lip. "Forgive me if my explanations are perhaps confused. I really do beg your pardon. Previously it was the

story ends p. 120

Commandant's habit to provide such explanations. But the New Commandant has excused himself from this honorable duty. The fact that with such an eminent visitor"—the traveler tried to deflect the honor with both hands, but the officer insisted on the expression—"that with such an eminent visitor he didn't even once make him aware of the form of our sentencing is yet again something new, which . . ." He had a curse on his lips, but controlled himself and said merely: "I was not informed about it. It's not my fault. In any case, I am certainly the person best able to explain our style of sentencing, for here I am carrying"—he patted his breast pocket—"the relevant diagrams drawn by the previous Commandant."

"Diagrams made by the Commandant himself?" asked the Traveler. "Then was he in his own person a combination of everything? Was he soldier, judge, engineer, chemist, and draftsman?"

"He was indeed," said the Officer, nodding his head with a fixed and thoughtful expression. Then he looked at his hands, examining them. They didn't seem to him clean enough to handle the diagrams. So he went to the bucket and washed them again. Then he pulled out a small leather folder and said, "Our sentence does not sound severe. The law which a condemned man has violated is inscribed on his body with the harrow. This Condemned Man, for example," and the Officer pointed to the man, "will have inscribed on his body, 'Honor your superiors.'"

The Traveler had a quick look at the man. When the Officer was pointing at him, the man kept his head down and appeared to be directing all his energy into listening in order to learn something. But the movements of his thick pouting lips showed clearly that he was incapable of understanding anything. The Traveler wanted to raise various questions, but after looking at the Condemned Man he merely asked, "Does he know his sentence?"

"No," said the Officer. He wished to get on with his explanation right away, but the Traveler interrupted him:

"He doesn't know his own sentence?"

"No," said the Officer once more. He then paused for a moment, as if he was asking the Traveler for a more detailed reason for his question, and said, "It would be useless to give him that information. He experiences it on his own body."

The Traveler really wanted to keep quiet at this point, but he felt how the Condemned Man was gazing at him—he seemed to be asking whether he could approve of the process the Officer had described. So the Traveler, who had up to this point been leaning back, bent forward again and kept up his questions, "But does he nonetheless have some general idea that he's been condemned?"

"Not that either," said the Officer, and he smiled at the traveler, as if he was still waiting for some strange revelations from him.

"No?" said the Traveler, wiping his forehead, "then does the man also not yet know how his defense was received?"

"He has had no opportunity to defend himself," said the Officer and looked away, as if he was talking to himself and wished not to embarrass the Traveler with an explanation of matters so self-evident to him.

"But he must have had a chance to defend himself," said the Traveler and stood up from his chair.

The Officer recognized that he was in danger of having his explanation of the apparatus held up for a long time. So he went to the Traveler, took him by the arm, pointed with his hand at the Condemned Man, who stood there stiffly now that the attention was so clearly directed at him—the Soldier was also pulling on his chain—and said, "The matter stands like this. Here in the penal colony I have been appointed judge. In spite of my youth. For I stood at the side of our Old Commandant in all matters of punishment, and I also know the most about the apparatus. The basic principle I use for my decisions is this: Guilt is always beyond a doubt. Other courts could not follow this principle, for they are made up of many heads and, in addition, have even higher courts above them. But that is not the case here, or at least it was not that way with the previous Commandant. It's true the

story ends p. 120

New Commandant has already shown a desire to get mixed up in my court, but I've succeeded so far in fending him off. And I'll continue to be successful. You want this case explained. It's simple—just like all of them. This morning a captain laid a charge that this man, who is assigned to him as a servant and who sleeps before his door, had been sleeping on duty. For his task is to stand up every time the clock strikes the hour and salute in front of the captain's door. That's certainly not a difficult duty—and it's necessary, since he is supposed to remain fresh both for guarding and for service. Yesterday night the captain wanted to check whether his servant was fulfilling his duty. He opened the door on the stroke of two and found him curled up asleep. He got his horsewhip and hit him across the face. Now, instead of standing up and begging for forgiveness, the man grabbed his master by the legs, shook him, and cried out, 'Throw away that whip or I'll eat you up.' Those are the facts. The captain came to me an hour ago. I wrote up his statement and right after that the sentence. Then I had the man chained up. It was all very simple. If I had first summoned the man and interrogated him, the result would have been confusion. He would have lied, and if I had been successful in refuting his lies, he would have replaced them with new lies, and so forth. But now I have him, and I won't release him again. Now, does that clarify everything? But time is passing. We should be starting the execution, and I haven't finished explaining the apparatus yet."

He urged the traveler to sit down in his chair, moved to the apparatus again, and started, "As you see, the shape of the harrow corresponds to the shape of a man. This is the harrow for the upper body, and here are the harrows for the legs. This small cutter is the only one designated for the head. Is that clear to you?" He leaned forward to the Traveler in a friendly way, ready to give the most comprehensive explanation.

The Traveler looked at the harrow with a wrinkled frown. The information about the judicial procedures had not satisfied him. However, he had to tell himself that here it was a matter of a penal colony, that in this place special regulations were necessary, and that one had to give precedence to military measures right down to the last detail. Beyond that, however, he had some hopes in the New Commandant, who obviously, although slowly, was intending to introduce a new procedure which the limited understanding of this Officer could not cope with.

Following this train of thought, the Traveler asked, "Will the Commandant be present at the execution?"

"That is not certain," said the Officer, embarrassingly affected by the sudden question, and his friendly expression made a grimace. "That's why we need to hurry up. As much as I regret the fact, I'll have to make my explanation even shorter. But tomorrow, once the apparatus is clean again—the fact that it gets so very dirty is its only fault—I could add a detailed explanation. So now, only the most important things. When the man is lying on the bed and it starts quivering, the harrow sinks onto the body. It positions itself automatically in such a way that it touches the body only lightly with the needle tips. Once the machine is set in this position, this steel cable tightens up into a rod. And now the performance begins. Someone who is not an initiate sees no external difference among the punishments. The harrow seems to do its work uniformly. As it quivers, it sticks the tips of its needles into the body, which is also vibrating from the movement of the bed. Now, to enable someone to check on how the sentence is being carried out, the harrow is made of glass. That gave rise to certain technical difficulties with fastening the needles securely, but after several attempts we were successful. We didn't spare any efforts. And now, as the inscription is made on the body, everyone can see through the glass. Don't you want to come closer and see the needles for yourself."

The Traveler stood slowly, moved up, and bent over the harrow.

"You see," the Officer said, "two sorts of needles in a multiple arrangement. Each long needle has a short one next to it. The long one inscribes, and the short one squirts water out to wash away the blood and keep the inscription always clear. The bloody

story ends p. 120

water is then channeled here in small grooves and finally flows into these main gutters, and the outlet pipe takes it to the pit." The officer pointed with his finger to the exact path which the bloody water had to take. As he began to demonstrate with both hands at the mouth of the outlet pipe, in order to make his account as clear as possible, the Traveler raised his head and, feeling behind him with his hand, wanted to return to his chair. Then he saw to his horror that the Condemned Man had also, like him, accepted the Officer's invitation to inspect the arrangement of the harrow up close. He had pulled the sleeping Soldier holding the chain a little forward and was also bending over the glass. One could see how with a confused gaze he also was looking for what the two gentlemen had just observed, but how he didn't succeed because he lacked the explanation. He leaned forward this way and that. He kept running his eyes over the glass again and again. The Traveler wanted to push him back, for what he was doing was probably punishable. But the Officer held the Traveler firmly with one hand, and with the other he took a lump of earth from the wall and threw it at the Soldier. The latter opened his eyes with a start, saw what the Condemned Man had dared to do, let his weapon fall, braced his heels in the earth, and pulled the Condemned Man back, so that he immediately collapsed. The Soldier looked down at him, as he writhed around, making his chain clink. "Stand him up," cried the Officer. Then he noticed that the Condemned Man was distracting the Traveler too much. The latter was even leaning out away from the harrow, without paying any attention to it, wanting to find out what was happening to the Condemned Man. "Handle him carefully," the Officer yelled again. He ran around the apparatus, personally grabbed the Condemned Man under the armpits and, with the help of the Soldier, stood the man, whose feet kept slipping, upright.

"Now I know all about it," said the Traveler, as the Officer turned back to him again.

"Except the most important thing," said the latter, grabbing the Traveler by the arm and pointing up high. "There in the inscriber is the mechanism which determines the movement of the harrow, and this mechanism is arranged according to the diagram on which the sentence is set down. I still use the diagrams of the previous Commandant. Here they are." He pulled some pages out of the leather folder. "Unfortunately I can't hand them to you. They are the most cherished thing I possess. Sit down, and I'll show you them from this distance. Then you'll be able to see it all well." He showed the first sheet. The Traveler would have been happy to say something appreciative, but all he saw was a labyrinthine series of lines, criss-crossing each other in all sort of ways. These covered the paper so thickly that only with difficulty could one make out the white spaces in between. "Read it," said the Officer.

"I can't," said the Traveler.

"But it's clear," said the Officer."

"It's very elaborate," said the Traveler evasively, "but I can't decipher it."

"Yes," said the Officer, smiling and putting the folder back again, "it's not calligraphy for school children. One has to read it a long time. You too will finally understand it clearly. Of course, it has to be a script that isn't simple. You see, it's not supposed to kill right away, but on average over a period of twelve hours. The turning point is set for the sixth hour. There must also be many, many embellishments surrounding the basic script. The essential script moves around the body only in a narrow belt. The rest of the body is reserved for decoration. Can you now appreciate the work of the harrow and the whole apparatus? Just look at it!" He jumped up the ladder, turned a wheel, and called down, "Watch out—move to the side!" Everything started moving. If the wheel had not squeaked, it would have been marvelous. The Officer threatened the wheel with his fist, as if he was surprised by the disturbance it created. Then he spread his arms, apologizing to the Traveler, and quickly clambered down, in order to observe the operation of the apparatus from below.

story ends p. 120

Something was still not working properly, something only he noticed. He clambered up again and reached with both hands into the inside of the inscriber. Then, in order to descend more quickly, instead of using the ladder, he slid down on one of the poles and, to make himself understandable through the noise, strained his voice to the limit as he yelled in the traveler's ear, "Do you understand the process? The harrow is starting to write. When it's finished with the first part of the script on the man's back, the layer of cotton wool rolls and turns the body slowly onto its side to give the harrow a new area. Meanwhile those parts lacerated by the inscription are lying on the cotton wool which, because it has been specially treated, immediately stops the bleeding and prepares the script for a further deepening. Here, as the body continues to rotate, prongs on the edge of the harrow then pull the cotton wool from the wounds, throw it into the pit, and the harrow goes to work again. In this way it keeps making the inscription deeper for twelve hours. For the first six hours the condemned man goes on living almost as before. He suffers nothing but pain. After two hours, the felt is removed, for at that point the man has no more energy for screaming. Here at the head of the bed warm rice pudding is put in this electrically heated bowl. From this the man, if he feels like it, can help himself to what he can lap up with his tongue. No one passes up this opportunity. I don't know of a single one, and I have had a lot of experience. He first loses his pleasure in eating around the sixth hour. I usually kneel down at this point and observe the phenomenon. The man rarely swallows the last bit. He turns it around in his mouth and spits it into the pit. When he does that, I have to lean aside or else he'll get me in the face. But how quiet the man becomes around the sixth hour! The most stupid of them begin to understand. It starts around the eyes and spreads out from there. A look that could tempt one to lie down under the harrow. Nothing else happens. The man simply begins to decipher the inscription. He purses his lips, as if he is listening. You've seen that it's not easy to figure out the inscription with your eyes, but our man deciphers it with his wounds. True, it takes a lot of work. It requires six hours to complete. But then the harrow spits him right out and throws him into the pit, where he splashes down into the bloody water and cotton wool. Then the judgment is over, and we, the soldier and I, quickly bury him."

The Traveler had leaned his ear toward the Officer and, with his hands in his coat pockets, was observing the machine at work. The Condemned Man was also watching, but without understanding. He bent forward a little and followed the moving needles, as the Soldier, after a signal from the Officer, cut through his shirt and trousers with a knife from the back, so that they fell off the Condemned Man. He wanted to grab the falling garments to cover his bare flesh, but the Soldier held him up and shook the last rags from him. The Officer turned the machine off, and in the silence which then ensued the Condemned Man was laid out under the harrow. The chains were taken off and the straps fastened in their place. For the Condemned Man it seemed at first glance to signify almost a relief. And now the harrow sunk down a stage lower, for the Condemned was a thin man. As the needle tips touched him, a shudder went over his skin. While the Soldier was busy with the right hand, the Condemned Man stretched out his left, with no sense of its direction. But it was pointing to where the Traveler was standing. The Officer kept looking at the Traveler from the side, without taking his eyes off him, as if he was trying to read from his face the impression he was getting of the execution, which he had now explained to him, at least superficially.

The strap meant to hold the wrist ripped off. The Soldier probably had pulled on it too hard. The Soldier showed the Officer the torn-off piece of strap, wanting him to help. So the Officer went over to him and said, with his face turned toward the Traveler, "The machine is very complicated. Now and then something has to tear or break. One shouldn't let that detract from one's overall opinion. Anyway, we have an immediate replacement for the strap. I'll use a chain—even though that will

story ends p. 120

affect the sensitivity of the movements for the right arm." And while he put the chain in place, he kept talking, "Our resources for maintaining the machine are very limited at the moment. Under the previous Commandant, I had free access to a cash box specially set aside for this purpose. There was a store room here in which all possible replacement parts were kept. I admit I made almost extravagant use of it. I mean earlier, not now, as the New Commandant claims. For him everything serves only as a pretext to fight against the old arrangements. Now he keeps the cash box for machinery under his own control, and if I ask him for a new strap, he demands the torn one as a piece of evidence, the new one doesn't arrive for ten days, and it's an inferior brand, of not much use to me. But how I am supposed to get the machine to work in the meantime without a strap—no one's concerned about that."

The Traveler was thinking: it's always questionable to intervene decisively in strange circumstances. He was neither a citizen of the penal colony nor a citizen of the state to which it belonged. If he wanted to condemn the execution or even hinder it, people could say to him: You're a foreigner—keep quiet. He would have nothing in response to that, but could only add that he did not understand what he was doing on this occasion, for the purpose of his traveling was merely to observe and not to alter other people's judicial systems in any way. True, at this point the way things were turning out it was very tempting. The injustice of the process and the inhumanity of the execution were beyond doubt. No one could assume that the Traveler was acting out of any sense of his own self-interest, for the Condemned Man was a stranger to him, not a countryman and not someone who invited sympathy in any way. The Traveler himself had letters of reference from high officials and had been welcomed here with great courtesy. The fact that he had been invited to this execution even seemed to indicate that people were asking for his judgment of this trial. This was all the more likely since the Commandant, as he had now heard only too clearly, was no supporter of this process and maintained an almost hostile relationship with the Officer.

Then the Traveler heard a cry of rage from the Officer. He had just shoved the stub of felt in the Condemned Man's mouth, not without difficulty, when the Condemned Man, overcome by an irresistible nausea, shut his eyes and threw up. The Officer quickly yanked him up off the stump and wanted to turn his head aside toward the pit. But it was too late. The vomit was already flowing down onto the machine. "This is all the Commandant's fault!" cried the Officer and mindlessly rattled the brass rods at the front. "My machine's as filthy as a pigsty." With trembling hands he showed the Traveler what had happened. "Haven't I spent hours trying to make the Commandant understand that a day before the execution there should be no more food served. But the new lenient administration has a different opinion. Before the man is led away, the Commandant's women cram sugary things down his throat. His whole life he's fed himself on stinking fish, and now he has to eat sweets! But that would be all right—I'd have no objections—but why don't they get a new felt, the way I've been asking him for three months now? How can anyone take this felt into his mouth without feeling disgusted—something that a hundred men have sucked and bitten on it as they were dying?"

The Condemned Man had laid his head down and appeared peaceful. The Soldier was busy cleaning up the machine with the Condemned Man's shirt. The Officer went up to the Traveler, who, feeling some premonition, took a step backward. But the Officer grasped him by the hand and pulled him aside. "I want to speak a few words to you in confidence," he said. "May I do that?"

"Of course," said the Traveler and listened with his eyes lowered.

"This process and execution, which you now have an opportunity to admire, have no more open supporters in our colony. I am its only defender, just as I am the single advocate for the legacy of the Old Commandant. I can no longer think about a

story ends p. 120

more extensive organization of the process—I'm using all my powers to maintain what there is at present. When the Old Commandant was alive, the colony was full of his supporters. I have something of the Old Commandant's power of persuasion, but I completely lack his power, and as a result the supporters have gone into hiding. There are still a lot of them, but no one admits to it. If you go into a tea house today—that is to say, on a day of execution—and keep your ears open, perhaps you'll hear nothing but ambiguous remarks. They are all supporters, but under the present Commandant, considering his present views, they are totally useless to me. And now I'm asking you: Should such a life's work," he pointed to the machine, "come to nothing because of this Commandant and the women influencing him? Should people let that happen? Even if one is a foreigner and only on our island for a couple of days? But there's no time to lose. People are already preparing something against my judicial proceedings. Discussions are already taking place in the Commandant's headquarters, to which I am not invited. Even your visit today seems to me typical of the whole situation. People are cowards and send you out—a foreigner. You should have seen the executions in earlier days! The entire valley was overflowing with people, even a day before the execution. They all came merely to watch. Early in the morning the Commandant appeared with his women. Fanfares woke up the entire campsite. I delivered the news that everything was ready. The whole society—and every high official had to attend—arranged itself around the machine. This pile of cane chairs is a sorry leftover from that time. The machine was freshly cleaned and glowed. For almost every execution I had new replacement parts. In front of hundreds of eyes—all the spectators stood on tiptoe right up to the hills there—the condemned man was laid down under the harrow by the Commandant himself. What nowadays is done by a common soldier was then my work as the senior judge, and it was an honor for me. And then the execution began! No discordant note disturbed the work of the machine. Many people did not look anymore at all, but lay down with closed eyes in the sand. They all knew: now justice was being carried out. In silence people listened to nothing but the groans of the condemned man, muffled by the felt. These days the machine no longer manages to squeeze a strong groan out of the condemned man—something the felt is not capable of smothering. But back then the needles which made the inscription dripped a caustic liquid which we are not permitted to use anymore today. Well, then came the sixth hour. It was impossible to grant all the requests people made to be allowed to watch from up close. The Commandant, in his wisdom, arranged that the children should be taken care of before all the rest. Naturally, I was always allowed to stand close by, because of my official position. Often I crouched down there with two small children in my arms, on my right and left. How we all took in the expression of transfiguration on the martyred face! How we held our cheeks in the glow of this justice, finally attained and already passing away! What times we had, my friend!"

The Officer had obviously forgotten who was standing in front of him. He had put his arm around the Traveler and laid his head on his shoulder. The Traveler was extremely embarrassed. Impatiently he looked away over the Officer's head. The Soldier had ended his task of cleaning and had just shaken some rice pudding into the bowl from a tin. No sooner had the Condemned Man, who seemed to have fully recovered already, noticed this than his tongue began to lick at the pudding. The Soldier kept pushing him away, for the pudding was probably meant for a later time, but in any case it was not proper for the Soldier to reach in and grab some food with his dirty hands and eat it in front of the famished Condemned Man.

The Officer quickly collected himself. "I didn't want to upset you in any way," he said. "I know it is impossible to make someone understand those days now. Besides, the machine still works and operates on its own. It operates on its own even when it is standing alone in this valley. And at the end, the body still keeps

story ends p. 120

falling in that incredibly soft flight into the pit, even if hundreds of people are not gathered like flies around the hole the way they used to be. Back then we had to erect a strong railing around the pit. It was pulled out long ago."

The Traveler wanted to turn his face away from the Officer and looked aimlessly around him. The Officer thought he was looking at the wasteland of the valley. So he grabbed his hands, turned him around in order to catch his gaze, and asked, "Do you see the shame of it?"

But the Traveler said nothing. The Officer left him alone for a while. With his legs apart and his hands on his hips, the Officer stood still and looked at the ground. Then he smiled at the Traveler cheerfully and said, "Yesterday I was nearby when the Commandant invited you. I heard the invitation. I know the Commandant. I understood right away what he intended with his invitation. Although his power might be sufficiently great to take action against me, he doesn't yet dare to. But my guess is that with you he is exposing me to the judgment of a respected foreigner. He calculates things with care. You are now in your second day on the island. You didn't know the Old Commandant and his way of thinking. You are trapped in a European way of seeing things. Perhaps you are fundamentally opposed to the death penalty in general and to this kind of mechanical style of execution in particular. Moreover, you see how the execution is a sad procedure, without any public participation, using a partially damaged machine. Now, if we take all this together (so the Commandant thinks) surely one could easily imagine that you would not consider my procedure proper? And if you didn't consider it right, you wouldn't keep quiet about it—I'm still speaking the mind of the Commandant—for you no doubt have faith that your tried-and-true convictions are correct. It's true that you have seen many peculiar things among many peoples and have learned to respect them. Thus, you will probably not speak out against the procedure with your full power, as you would perhaps in your own homeland. But the Commandant doesn't really need that. A casual word, merely a careless remark, is enough. It doesn't have to match your convictions at all, so long as it corresponds to his wishes. I'm certain he will use all his shrewdness to interrogate you. And his women will sit around in a circle and perk up their ears. You will say something like, 'Among us the judicial procedures are different,' or 'With us the accused is questioned before the verdict,' or 'We had torture only in the Middle Ages.' For you these observations appear as correct as they are self-evident—innocent remarks which do not impugn[4] my procedure. But how will the Commandant take them? I see him, our excellent Commandant—the way he immediately pushes his stool aside and hurries out to the balcony—I see his women, how they stream after him. I hear his voice—the women call it a thunder voice. And now he's speaking: 'A great Western explorer who has been commissioned to inspect judicial procedures in all countries has just said that our process based on old customs is inhuman. After the verdict of such a personality it is, of course, no longer possible for me to tolerate this procedure. So from this day on I am ordering . . . and so forth.' You want to intervene—you didn't say what he is reporting—you didn't call my procedure inhuman; by contrast, in keeping with your deep insight, you consider it most humane and most worthy of human beings. You also admire this machinery. But it is too late. You don't even go onto the balcony, which is already filled with women. You want to attract attention. You want to cry out. But a lady's hand is covering your mouth, and I and the Old Commandant's work are lost."

The Traveler had to suppress a smile. So the work which he had considered so difficult was easy. He said evasively, "You're exaggerating my influence. The Commandant has read my letters of recommendation. He knows that I am no expert in judicial processes. If I were to express an opinion, it would be that of a lay person, no more significant than the opinion of anyone

[4] Cast doubt upon; call into question.

story ends p. 120

else, and in any case far less significant than the opinion of the Commandant, who, as I understand it, has very extensive powers in this penal colony. If his views of this procedure are as definite as you think they are, then I'm afraid the time has come for this procedure to end, without any need for my humble opinion."

Did the Officer understand by now? No, he did not yet get it. He shook his head vigorously, briefly looked back at the Condemned Man and the Soldier, who both flinched and stopped eating the rice, went up really close up to the Traveler, without looking into his face, but gazing at parts of his jacket, and said more gently than before: "You don't know the Commandant. Where he and all of us are concerned you are—forgive the expression—to a certain extent innocent. Your influence, believe me, cannot be overestimated. In fact, I was blissfully happy when I heard that you were to be present at the execution by yourself. This order of the Commandant was aimed at me, but now I'll turn it to my advantage. Without being distracted by false insinuations and disparaging looks—which could not have been avoided with a greater number of participants at the execution—you have listened to my explanation, looked at the machine, and are now about to view the execution. Your verdict is no doubt already fixed. If some small uncertainties remain, witnessing the execution will remove them. And now I'm asking you—help me with the Commandant!"

The Traveler did not let him go on talking. "How can I do that," he cried. "It's totally impossible. I can help you as little as I can harm you."

"You could do it," said the Officer. With some apprehension the Traveler observed that the Officer was clenching his fists. "You could do it," repeated the Officer, even more emphatically. "I have a plan which must succeed. You think your influence is insufficient. I know it will be enough. But assuming you're right, doesn't saving this whole procedure require one to try even those methods which may be inadequate? So listen to my plan. To carry it out, it's necessary, above all, for you to keep as quiet as possible today in the colony about your verdict on this procedure. Unless someone asks you directly, you should not express any view whatsoever. But what you do say must be short and vague. People should notice that it's difficult for you to speak about the subject, that you feel bitter, that, if you were to speak openly, you'd have to burst out cursing on the spot. I'm not asking you to lie, not at all. You should only give brief answers—something like, 'Yes, I've seen the execution' or 'Yes, I've heard the full explanation.' That's all—nothing further. For that will be enough of an indication for people to observe in you a certain bitterness, even if that's not what the Commandant will think. Naturally, he will completely misunderstand the issue and interpret it in his own way. My plan is based on that. Tomorrow a large meeting of all the higher administrative officials takes place at headquarters under the chairmanship of the Commandant. He, of course, understands how to turn such a meeting into a spectacle. A gallery has been built, which is always full of spectators. I'm compelled to take part in the discussions, though they fill me with disgust. In any case, you will certainly be invited to the meeting. If you follow my plan today and behave accordingly, the invitation will become an emphatic request. But should you for some inexplicable reason still not be invited, you must make sure you request an invitation. Then you'll receive one without question. Now, tomorrow you are sitting with the women in the commandant's box. With frequent upward glances he reassures himself that you are there. After various trivial and ridiculous agenda items designed for the spectators—mostly harbor construction—always harbor construction—the judicial process comes up for discussion. If it's not raised by the Commandant himself or does not occur soon enough, I'll make sure that it comes up. I'll stand up and report on today's execution. Really briefly—just the report. Such a report is not really customary; however, I'll do it, nonetheless. The Commandant thanks me, as always, with a friendly smile. And now he cannot restrain himself. He seizes this excellent opportunity. 'The report of the execution,' he'll say, or something

story ends p. 120

like that, 'has just been given. I would like to add to this report only the fact that this particular execution was attended by the great explorer whose visit confers such extraordinary honor on our colony, as you all know. Even the significance of our meeting today has been increased by his presence. Should we not now ask this great explorer for his appraisal of the execution based on old customs and of the process which preceded it?' Of course, there is the noise of applause everywhere, universal agreement. And I'm louder than anyone. The Commandant bows before you and says, 'Then in everyone's name, I'm putting the question to you.' And now you step up to the railing. Place your hands where everyone can see them. Otherwise the ladies will grab them and play with your fingers. And now finally come your remarks. I don't know how I'll bear the tension up to then. In your speech you mustn't hold back. Let truth resound. Lean over the railing and shout it out—yes, yes, roar your opinion at the Commandant, your unshakable opinion. But perhaps you don't want to do that. It doesn't suit your character. Perhaps in your country people behave differently in such situations. That's all right. That's perfectly satisfactory. Don't stand up at all. Just say a couple of words. Whisper them so that only the officials underneath you can just hear them. That's enough. You don't even have to say anything at all about the lack of attendance at the execution or about the squeaky wheel, the torn strap, the disgusting felt. No. I'll take over all further details, and, believe me, if my speech doesn't chase him out of the room, it will force him to his knees, so he'll have to admit it: 'Old Commandant, I bow down before you.' That's my plan. Do you want to help me carry it out? But, of course, you want to. More than that—you have to."

And the officer gripped the Traveler by both arms and looked at him, breathing heavily into his face. He had yelled the last sentences so loudly that even the Soldier and the Condemned Man were paying attention. Although they couldn't understand a thing, they stopped eating and looked over at the Traveler, still chewing.

From the start the Traveler had had no doubts about the answer he must give. He had experienced too much in his life to be able to waver here. Basically he was honest and unafraid. Still, with the Soldier and the Condemned Man looking at him, he hesitated a moment. But finally he said, as he had to, "No." The Officer's eyes blinked several times, but he did not take his eyes off the Traveler. "Would you like an explanation," asked the Traveler. The Officer nodded dumbly. "I am opposed to this procedure," said the Traveler. "Even before you took me into your confidence—and, of course, I will never abuse your confidence under any circumstances—I was already thinking about whether I was entitled to intervene against this procedure and whether my intervention could have the smallest chance of success. And if that was the case, it was clear to me whom I had to turn to first of all—naturally, to the Commandant. You clarified the issue for me even more, but without reinforcing my decision in any way—quite the reverse. I find your conviction genuinely moving, even if it cannot deter me."

The Officer remained quiet, turned toward the machine, grabbed one of the brass rods, and then, leaning back a little, looked up at the inscriber, as if he was checking that everything was in order. The Soldier and the Condemned Man seemed to have made friends with each other. The Condemned Man was making signs to the Soldier, although, given the tight straps on him, this was difficult for him to do. The Soldier was leaning into him. The Condemned Man whispered something to him, and the Soldier nodded. The Traveler went over to the Officer and said, "You don't yet know what I'll do. Yes, I will tell the Commandant my opinion of the procedure—not in a meeting, but in private. In addition, I won't stay here long enough to be able to get called into some meeting or other. Early tomorrow morning I leave, or at least I go on board ship."

It didn't look as if the Officer had been listening. "So the process has not convinced you," he said to himself, smiling the way an old man smiles over the silliness of a child, concealing his own true thoughts behind that smile.

"Well then, it's time," he said finally and suddenly looked at the Traveler with bright eyes which contained some sort of demand, some appeal for participation.

"Time for what?" asked the Traveler uneasily. But there was no answer.

"You are free," the Officer told the Condemned Man in his own language. At first the man did not believe him. "You are free now," said the Officer. For the first time the face of the Condemned Man showed signs of real life. Was it the truth? Was it only the Officer's mood, which could change? Had the foreign Traveler brought him a reprieve? What was it? That's what the man's face seemed to be asking. But not for long. Whatever the case might be, if he could he wanted to be truly free, and he began to shake back and forth, as much as the harrow permitted.

"You're tearing my straps," cried the Officer. "Be still! We'll undo them right away." And, giving a signal to the Soldier, he set to work with him. The Condemned Man said nothing and smiled slightly to himself. He turned his face to the Officer and then to the Soldier and then back again, without ignoring the Traveler.

"Pull him out," the Officer ordered the Soldier. This process required a certain amount of care because of the harrow. The Condemned Man already had a few small wounds on his back, thanks to his own impatience.

From this point on, however, the Officer paid him hardly any attention. He went up to the Traveler, pulled out the small leather folder once more, leafed through it, finally found the sheet he was looking for, and showed it to the Traveler. "Read that," he said.

"I can't," said the Traveler. "I've already told you I can't read these pages."

"But take a close look at the page," said the Officer, and moved up right next to the Traveler in order to read with him. When that didn't help, he raised his little finger high up over the paper, as if the page must not be touched under any circumstances, so that using this he might make the task of reading easier for the Traveler. The Traveler also made an effort so that at least he could satisfy the Officer, but it was impossible for him. Then the Officer began to spell out the inscription and then read out once again the joined up letters. "'Be just!' it states," he said. "Now you can read it." The Traveler bent so low over the paper that the Officer, afraid that he might touch it, moved it further away. The Traveler didn't say anything more, but it was clear that he was still unable to read anything. " 'Be just!' it says," the Officer remarked once again.

"That could be," said the Traveler. "I do believe that's written there."

"Good," said the Officer, at least partially satisfied. He climbed up the ladder, holding the paper. With great care he set the page in the inscriber and appeared to rotate the gear mechanism completely around. This was very tiring work. It must have required him to deal with extremely small wheels. He had to inspect the gears so closely that sometimes his head disappeared completely into the inscriber.

The Traveler followed this work from below without looking away. His neck grew stiff, and his eyes found the sunlight pouring down from the sky painful. The Soldier and the Condemned Man were keeping each other busy. With the tip of his bayonet the Soldier pulled out the Condemned Man's shirt and trousers which were lying in the hole. The shirt was horribly dirty, and the Condemned Man washed it in the bucket of water. When he was putting on his shirt and trousers, the Soldier and the Condemned Man had to laugh out loud, for the pieces of clothing were cut in two up the back. Perhaps the Condemned Man thought that it was his duty to amuse the Soldier. In his ripped-up clothes he circled around the Soldier, who crouched down on the ground, laughed, and slapped his knees. But they restrained themselves out of consideration for the two gentlemen present.

story ends p. 120

When the Officer was finally finished up on the machine, with a smile he looked over the whole thing and all its parts one more time, and this time closed the cover of the inscriber, which had been open up to this point. He climbed down, looked into the hole and then at the Condemned Man, observed with satisfaction that he had pulled out his clothes, then went to the bucket of water to wash his hands, recognized too late that it was disgustingly dirty, and was upset that now he couldn't wash his hands. Finally he pushed them into the sand. This option didn't satisfy him, but he had to do what he could in the circumstances. Then he stood up and began to unbutton the coat of his uniform. As he did this, the two lady's handkerchiefs, which he had pushed into the back of his collar, fell into his hands. "Here you have your handkerchiefs," he said and threw them over to the Condemned Man. And to the Traveler he said by way of an explanation, "Presents from the ladies."

In spite of the obvious speed with which he took off the coat of his uniform and then undressed himself completely, he handled each piece of clothing very carefully, even running his fingers over the silver braids on his tunic with special care and shaking a tassel into place. But in great contrast to this care, as soon he was finished handling an article of clothing, he immediately flung it angrily into the hole. The last items he had left were his short sword and its harness. He pulled the sword out of its scabbard, broke it in pieces, gathered up everything—the pieces of the sword, the scabbard, and the harness—and threw them away so forcefully that they rattled against each other down in the pit.

Now he stood there naked. The Traveler bit his lip and said nothing. For he was aware what would happen, but he had no right to hinder the Officer in any way. If the judicial process to which the officer clung was really so close to the point of being canceled—perhaps as a result of the intervention of the Traveler, something to which he for his part felt duty-bound—then the Officer was now acting in a completely correct manner. In his place, the Traveler would not have acted any differently.

The Soldier and the Condemned Man at first didn't understand a thing. To begin with they didn't look, not even once. The Condemned Man was extremely happy to get the handkerchiefs back, but he couldn't enjoy them very long, for the Soldier snatched them from him with a quick grab, which he had not anticipated. The Condemned Man then tried to pull the handkerchiefs out from the Soldier's belt, where he had put them for safe keeping, but the Soldier was too wary. So they were fighting, half in jest. Only when the Officer was fully naked did they start to pay attention. The Condemned Man especially seemed to be struck by a premonition of some sort of significant transformation. What had happened to him was now taking place with the Officer. Perhaps this time the procedure would play itself out to its conclusion. The foreign Traveler had probably given the order. So that was revenge. Without having suffered all the way to the end himself, nonetheless he would be completely revenged. A wide, silent laugh now appeared on his face and did not go away.

The Officer, however, had turned toward the machine. If earlier on it had already become clear that he understood the machine thoroughly, one might well get alarmed now at the way he handled it and how it obeyed. He only had to bring his hand near the harrow for it to rise and sink several times, until it had reached the correct position to make room for him. He only had to grasp the bed by the edges, and it already began to quiver. The stump of felt moved up to his mouth. One could see how the Officer really didn't want to accept it, but his hesitation was only momentary—he immediately submitted and took it in. Everything was ready, except that the straps still hung down on the sides. But they were clearly unnecessary. The Officer did not have to be strapped down. When the Condemned Man saw the loose straps, he thought the execution would be incomplete unless they were fastened. He waved eagerly to the Soldier, and they ran over to strap in the Officer. The latter had already stuck out his foot to kick the crank designed to set the inscriber in motion. Then he saw the two men coming. So he pulled his foot

story ends p. 120

back and let himself be strapped in. But now he could no longer reach the crank. Neither the Soldier nor the Condemned Man would find it, and the Traveler was determined not to touch it. But that was unnecessary. Hardly were the straps attached when the machine already started working. The bed quivered, the needles danced on his skin, and the harrow swung up and down. The Traveler had already been staring for some time before he remembered that a wheel in the inscriber was supposed to squeak. But everything was quiet, without the slightest audible hum.

Because of its silent working, the machine did not really attract attention. The Traveler looked over at the Soldier and the Condemned Man. The Condemned Man was the livelier of the two. Everything in the machine interested him. At times he bent down—at other times he stretched up, all the time pointing with his forefinger in order to show something to the Soldier. For the Traveler it was embarrassing. He was determined to remain here until the end, but he could no longer endure the sight of the two men. "Go home," he said. The Soldier might have been ready to do that, but the Condemned Man took the order as a direct punishment. With his hands folded he begged and pleaded to be allowed to stay there. And when the Traveler shook his head and was unwilling to give in, he even knelt down. Seeing that orders were of no help here, the Traveler wanted to go over and chase the two away.

Then he heard a noise from up in the inscriber. He looked up. So was the gear wheel going out of alignment? But it was something else. The lid on the inscriber was lifting up slowly. Then it fell completely open. The teeth of a cog wheel were exposed and lifted up. Soon the entire wheel appeared. It was as if some huge force was compressing the inscriber, so that there was no longer sufficient room for this wheel. The wheel rolled all the way to the edge of the inscriber, fell down, rolled upright a bit in the sand, and then fell over and lay still. But already up on the inscriber another gear wheel was moving upward. Several others followed—large ones, small ones, ones hard to distinguish. With each of them the same thing happened. One kept thinking that now the inscriber must surely be empty, but then a new cluster with lots of parts would move up, fall down, roll in the sand, and lie still. With all this going on, the Condemned Man totally forgot the Traveler's order. The gear wheels completely delighted him. He kept wanting to grab one, and at the same time he was urging the Soldier to help him. But he kept pulling his hand back startled, for immediately another wheel followed, which, at least in its initial rolling, surprised him.

The Traveler, by contrast, was very upset. Obviously the machine was breaking up. Its quiet operation had been an illusion. He felt as if he had to look after the Officer, now that the latter could no longer look after himself. But while the falling gear wheels were claiming all his attention, he had neglected to look at the rest of the machine. However, when he now bent over the harrow, once the last gear wheel had left the inscriber, he had a new, even more unpleasant surprise. The harrow was not writing but only stabbing, and the bed was not rolling the body, but lifting it, quivering, up into the needles. The Traveler wanted to reach in to stop the whole thing, if possible. This was not the torture the Officer wished to attain. It was murder, pure and simple. He stretched out his hands. But at that point the harrow was already moving upward and to the side, with the skewered body—just as it did in other cases, but only in the twelfth hour. Blood flowed out in hundreds of streams, not mixed with water—the water tubes had also failed to work this time. Then one last thing went wrong: the body would not come loose from the needles. Its blood streamed out, but it hung over the pit without falling. The harrow wanted to move back to its original position, but, as if it realized that it could not free itself of its load, it remained over the hole.

"Help," the Traveler yelled out to the Soldier and the Condemned Man and grabbed the Officer's feet. He wanted to push against the feet himself and have the two others grab the Officer's head from the other side, so he could be slowly taken off the

story ends p. 120

needles. But now the two men could not make up their mind whether to come or not. The Condemned Man turned away at once. The Traveler had to go over to him and drag him to the Officer's head by force. At this point, almost against his will, he looked at the face of the corpse. It was as it had been in his life. He could discover no sign of the promised transfiguration. What all the others had found in the machine, the Officer had not. His lips were pressed firmly together, his eyes were open and looked as they had when he was alive, his gaze was calm and convinced. The tip of a large iron needle had gone through his forehead.

As the Traveler, with the Soldier and the Condemned Man behind him, came to the first houses in the colony, the Soldier pointed to one and said, "That's the tea house."

On the ground floor of one of the houses was a deep, low room, like a cave, with smoke-covered walls and ceiling. On the street side it was open along its full width. Although there was little difference between the tea house and the rest of the houses in the colony, which were all very dilapidated, except for the Commandant's palatial structure, the Traveler was struck by the impression of historical memory, and he felt the power of earlier times. Followed by his companions, he walked closer, going between the unoccupied tables, which stood in the street in front of the tea house, and took a breath of the cool, stuffy air which came from inside. "The old man is buried here," said the soldier; "a place in the cemetery was denied him by the chaplain. For a long time people were undecided where they should bury him. Finally they buried him here. Of course, the Officer explained none of that to you, for naturally he was the one most ashamed about it. A few times he even tried to dig up the old man at night, but he was always chased off."

"Where is the grave?" asked the Traveler, who could not believe the Soldier. Instantly both men, the Soldier and the Condemned Man, ran in front of him and with hands outstretched pointed to the place where the grave was located. They led the Traveler to the back wall, where guests were sitting at a few tables. They were presumably dock workers, strong men with short, shiny, black beards. None of them wore coats, and their shirts were torn. They were poor, oppressed people. As the Traveler came closer, a few got up, leaned against the wall, and looked at him. A whisper went up around the Traveler—"It's a foreigner. He wants to look at the grave." They pushed one of the tables aside, under which there was a real grave stone. It was a simple stone, low enough for it to remain hidden under a table. It bore an inscription in very small letters. In order to read it the Traveler had to kneel down. It read, "Here rests the Old Commandant. His followers, who are now not permitted to have a name, buried him in this grave and erected this stone. There exists a prophecy that the Commandant will rise again after a certain number of years and from this house will lead his followers to a re-conquest of the colony. Have faith and wait!"

When the Traveler had read it and got up, he saw the men standing around him and smiling, as if they had read the inscription with him, found it ridiculous, and were asking him to share their opinion. The Traveler acted as if he hadn't noticed, distributed some coins among them, waited until the table was pushed back over the grave, left the tea house, and went to the harbor.

In the tea house the Soldier and the Condemned Man had come across some people they knew who detained them. However, they must have broken free of them soon, because by the time the Traveler found himself in the middle of a long staircase which led to the boats, they were already running after him. They probably wanted to force the Traveler at the last minute to take them with him. While the Traveler was haggling at the bottom of the stairs with a sailor about his passage out to the steamer, the two men were racing down the steps in

story ends next p.

silence, for they didn't dare cry out. But as they reached the bottom, the Traveler was already in the boat, and the sailor at once cast off from shore. They could still have jumped into the boat, but the Traveler picked up a heavy knotted rope from the boat bottom, threatened them with it, and thus prevented them from jumping in.

UP IN THE GALLERY

If some frail tubercular lady circus rider were to be driven in circles around and around the arena for months and months without interruption in front of a tireless public on a swaying horse by a merciless whip-wielding master of ceremonies, spinning on the horse, throwing kisses and swaying at the waist, and if this performance, amid the incessant roar of the orchestra and the ventilators, were to continue into the ever-expanding, gray future, accompanied by applause, which died down and then swelled up again, from hands which were really steam hammers, perhaps then a young visitor to the gallery might rush down the long staircase through all the levels, burst into the ring, and cry "Stop!" through the fanfares of the constantly adjusting orchestra.

But since things are not like that—since a beautiful woman, in white and red, flies in through curtains which proud men in livery open in front of her, since the director, devotedly seeking her eyes, breathes in her direction, behaving like an animal, and, as a precaution, lifts her up on the dapple-gray horse, as if she were his granddaughter, the one he loved more than anything else, as she starts a dangerous journey, but he cannot decide to give the signal with his whip and finally, controlling himself, gives it a crack, runs right beside the horse with his mouth open, follows the rider's leaps with a sharp gaze, hardly capable of comprehending her skill, tries to warn her by calling out in English, furiously castigating[1] the grooms holding hoops, telling them to pay the most scrupulous attention, and begs the orchestra, with upraised arms, to be quiet before the great jump, finally lifts the small woman down from the trembling horse, kisses her on both cheeks, considers no public tribute adequate, while she herself, leaning on him, high on the tips of her toes, with dust swirling around her, arms outstretched and head thrown back, wants to share her luck with the entire circus—since this is how things are, the visitor to the gallery puts his face on the railing and, sinking into the final march as if into a difficult dream, weeps, without realizing it.

---

[1] To reprimand, criticize, or rebuke severely.

JACKALS AND ARABS

We were camping in the oasis. My companions were asleep. An Arab, tall and dressed in white, went past me. He had been tending to his camels and was going to his sleeping place.

I threw myself on my back into the grass. I wanted to sleep. I couldn't. The howling of a jackal in the distance—I sat up straight again. And what had been so far away was suddenly close by. A swarming pack of jackals around me, their eyes flashing dull gold and going out, slender bodies moving in a quick, coordinated manner, as if responding to a whip.

One of them came from behind, pushed himself under my arm, right against me, as if it needed my warmth, then stepped in front of me and spoke, almost eye to eye with me.

"I'm the oldest jackal for miles around. I'm happy I'm still able to welcome you here. I had already almost given up hope, for we've been waiting for you an infinitely long time. My mother waited, and her mother, and all her mothers, right back to the mother of all jackals. Believe me!"

"That surprises me," I said, forgetting to light the pile of wood which lay ready to keep the jackals away with its smoke, "I'm very surprised to hear that. I've come from the high north merely by chance and am in the middle of a short trip. What do you jackals want then?"

As if encouraged by this conversation, which was perhaps

too friendly, they drew their circle more closely around me, all panting and snarling.

"We know," the oldest began, "that you come from the north. Our hope rests on that very point. In the north there is a way of understanding things which one cannot find here among the Arabs. You know, from their cool arrogance one cannot strike a spark of common sense. They kill animals to eat them, and they disregard rotting carcasses."

"Don't speak so loud," I said. "There are Arabs sleeping close by."

"You really are a stranger," said the jackal. "Otherwise you would know that throughout the history of the world a jackal has never yet feared an Arab. Should we fear them? Is it not misfortune enough that we have been cast out among such people?"

"Maybe—that could be," I said. "I'm not up to judging things which are so far removed from me. It seems to be a very old conflict—it's probably in the blood and so perhaps will only end with blood."

"You are very clever" said the old jackal, and they all panted even more quickly, their lungs breathing rapidly, although they were standing still. A bitter smell streamed out of their open jaws—at times I could tolerate it only by clenching my teeth. "You are very clever. What you said corresponds to our ancient doctrine. So we take their blood, and the quarrel is over."

"Oh," I said, more sharply than I intended, "they'll defend themselves. They'll shoot you down in droves with their guns."

"You do not understand us," he said, "a characteristic of human beings which has not disappeared, not even in the high north. We are not going to kill them. The Nile would not have enough water to wash us clean. The very sight of their living bodies makes us run away immediately into cleaner air, into the desert, which, for that very reason, is our home."

All the jackals surrounding us—and in the meantime many more had come up from a distance—lowered their heads between the front legs and cleaned them with their paws. It was as if they wanted to conceal an aversion which was so terrible, that I would have much preferred to take a big jump and escape beyond their circle.

"So what do you intend to do," I asked. I wanted to stand up, but I couldn't. Two young animals were holding me firmly from behind with their jaws biting my jacket and shirt. I had to remain sitting. "They are holding your train,"[1] said the old jackal seriously, by way of explanation, "a mark of respect."

"They should let me go," I cried out, turning back and forth between the old one and the young ones.

"Of course, they will," said the old one, "if that's what you want. But it will take a little while, for, as is our habit, they have dug their teeth in deep and must first let their jaws open gradually. Meanwhile, listen to our request."

"Your conduct has not made me particularly receptive to it," I said.

"Don't make us pay for our clumsiness," he said, and now for the first time he brought the plaintive tone of his natural voice to his assistance. "We are poor animals—all we have is our teeth. For everything we want to do—good and bad—the only thing available to us is our teeth."

"So what do you want?" I asked, only slightly reassured.

"Sir," he cried out, and all the jackals howled. To me it sounded very remotely like a melody. "Sir, you should end the quarrel which divides the world in two. Our ancestors described a man like you as the one who will do it. We must be free of the Arabs—with air we can breathe, a view of the horizon around us clear of Arabs, no cries of pain from a sheep which an Arab has knifed, and every animal should die peacefully and be left undisturbed for us to drain it empty and clean it right down to the bones. Cleanliness—that's what we want—nothing but cleanliness." Now they were all crying and sobbing. "How can you bear it in this world, you noble heart and sweet entrails?

---

[1] An elongated or long piece of material attached to the back of clothing.

story ends next p.

Dirt is their white; dirt is their black; their beards are horrible; looking at the corner of their eyes makes one spit; and if they lift their arms, hell opens up in their armpits. And that's why, sir, that's why, my dear sir, with the help of your all-capable hands you must use these scissors to slit right through their throats." He jerked his head, and in response a jackal came up carrying on its canine tooth a small pair of sewing scissors covered with old rust.

"So finally the scissors—it's time to stop!" cried the Arab leader of our caravan, who had crept up on us from downwind. Now he swung his gigantic whip.

The jackals all fled quickly, but still remained at some distance huddled closely together, many animals so close and stiff that it looked as if they were in a narrow pen with jack o' lanterns flying around them.

"So, you too, sir, have seen and heard this spectacle," said the Arab, laughing as cheerfully as the reticence of his race permitted.

"So you know what the animals want," I asked.

"Of course, sir," he said. "That's common knowledge—as long as there are Arabs, these scissors will wander with us through the deserts until the end of days. Every European is offered them for the great work; every European is exactly the one they think qualified to do it. These animals have an absurd hope. They're idiots, real idiots. That's why we're fond of them. They are our dogs, finer than the ones you have. Now, watch this. In the night a camel died. I have had it brought here."

Four bearers came and threw the heavy carcass right in front of us. No sooner was it lying there than the jackals raised their voices. Every one of them crept forward, its body scraping the ground, as if drawn by an irresistible rope. They had forgotten the Arabs, forgotten their hatred. The presence of a powerfully stinking dead body wiped out everything and enchanted them. One of them was already hanging at the camel's throat and with its first bite had found the artery. Like a small angry pump which—with a determination matched only by its hopelessness—seeks to put out an overpowering fire, every muscle of its body pulled and twitched in its place. Then right away they were lying there on the corpse working in the same way, piled up like a mountain.

Then the leader cracked his sharp whip powerfully all around above them. They raised their heads, half fainting in their intoxicated state, looked at the Arab standing in front of them, started to feel the whip now hitting their muzzles, jumped away, and ran back a distance. But the camel's blood was already lying there in pools, stinking to heaven, and the body was torn wide open in several places. They could not resist. They were there again. The leader once more raised his whip. I grabbed his arm. "Sir, you are right," he said. "We'll leave them to their calling. Besides, it's time to break camp. You've seen them. Wonderful creatures, aren't they? And how they hate us!"

A COUNTRY DOCTOR

I was in great difficulty. An urgent journey was facing me. A seriously ill man was waiting for me in a village ten miles distant. A severe snowstorm filled the space between him and me. I had a carriage—a light one, with large wheels, entirely suitable for our country roads. Wrapped up in furs with the bag of instruments in my hand, I was already standing in the courtyard ready for the journey; but the horse was missing—the horse. My own horse had died the previous night, as a result of over exertion in this icy winter. My servant girl was at that very moment running around the village to see if she could borrow a horse, but it was hopeless—I knew that—and I stood there useless, increasingly covered with snow, becoming all the time more immobile. The girl appeared at the gate, alone. She was swinging the lantern. Of course, who is now going to lend her his horse for such a journey? I walked once again across the courtyard. I couldn't see what to do. Distracted and tormented, I kicked my foot against the cracked door of the pig sty which had not been used for years. The door opened and banged to and fro on its hinges. A warmth and smell as if from horses came out. A dim stall lantern on a rope swayed inside. A man huddled down in the stall below showed his open blue-eyed face. "Shall I hitch up?" he asked, crawling out on all fours. I didn't know what to say and bent down to see what was still in the stall. The servant girl stood beside me.

"One doesn't know the sorts of things one has stored in one's own house," she said, and we both laughed. "Hey, Brother, hey Sister," the groom[1] cried out, and two horses, powerful animals with strong flanks, shoved their way one behind the other, legs close to the bodies, lowering their well-formed heads like camels, and getting through the door space, which they completely filled, only through the powerful movements of their rumps. But right away they stood up straight, long legged, with thick steaming bodies. "Help him," I said, and the girl obediently hurried to hand the wagon harness to the groom. But as soon as she was beside him, the groom puts his arms around her and pushes his face against hers. She screams out and runs over to me. On the girl's cheek were red marks from two rows of teeth. "You brute," I cry out in fury, "do you want the whip?" But I immediately remember that he is a stranger, that I don't know where he comes from, and that he's helping me out of his own free will, when everyone else is refusing to. As if he knows what I was thinking, he takes no offense at my threat, but turns around to me once more, still busy with the horses. Then he says, "Climb in," and, in fact, everything is ready. I notice that I have never before traveled with such a beautiful team of horses, and I climb in happily. "But I'll take the reins. You don't know the way," I say. "Of course," he says; "I'm not going with you. I'm staying with Rosa."

"No," screams Rosa and runs into the house, with an accurate premonition of the inevitability of her fate. I hear the door chain rattling as she sets it in place. I hear the lock click. I see how in addition she runs down the corridor and through the rooms putting out all the lights in order to make herself impossible to find. "You're coming with me," I say to the groom, "or I'll give up the journey, no matter how urgent it is. It's not my intention to give you the girl as the price of the trip."

"Giddy up," he says and claps his hands. The carriage is torn away, like a piece of wood in a current. I still hear how the door

---

[1] One employed to care for horses and/or a stable.

of my house is breaking down and splitting apart under the groom's onslaught, and then my eyes and ears are filled with a roaring sound which overwhelms all my senses at once. But only for a moment. Then I am already there, as if the farm yard of my invalid opens up immediately in front of my courtyard gate. The horses stand quietly. The snowfall has stopped, moonlight all around. The sick man's parents rush out of the house, his sister behind them. They almost lift me out of the carriage. I get nothing from their confused talking. In the sick room one can hardly breathe the air. The neglected cooking stove is smoking. I want to push open the window, but first I'll look at the sick man. Thin, without fever, not cold, not warm, with empty eyes, without a shirt, the young man under the stuffed quilt heaves himself up, hangs around my throat, and whispers in my ear, "Doctor, let me die." I look around. No one has heard. The parents stand silently, leaning forward, and wait for my opinion. The sister has brought a stool for my handbag. I open the bag and look among my instruments. The young man constantly gropes at me from the bed to remind me of his request. I take some tweezers, test them in the candle light, and put them back. "Yes," I think blasphemously, "in such cases the gods do help. They send the missing horse, even add a second one because it's urgent, and even throw in a groom as a bonus." Now for the first time I think once more of Rosa. What am I doing? How am I saving her? How do I pull her out from under this groom, ten miles away from her, with uncontrollable horses in the front of my carriage? These horses, who have somehow loosened their straps, are pushing open the window from outside, I don't know how. Each one is sticking its head through a window and, unmoved by the crying of the family, is observing the invalid. "I'll go back right away," I think, as if the horses were ordering me to journey back, but I allow the sister, who thinks I am in a daze because of the heat, to take off my fur coat. A glass of rum is prepared for me. The old man claps me on the shoulder; the sacrifice of his treasure justifies this familiarity. I shake my head. In the narrow circle

story ends p. 135

of the old man's thinking I was not well; that's the only reason I refuse to drink. The mother stands by the bed and entices me over. I follow and, as a horse neighs loudly at the ceiling, lay my head on the young man's chest, which trembles under my wet beard. That confirms what I know: the young man is healthy. His circulation is a little off, saturated with coffee by his caring mother, but he's healthy and best pushed out of bed with a shove. I'm no improver of the world and let him lie there. I am employed by the district and do my duty to the full, right to the point where it's almost too much. Badly paid, but I'm generous and ready to help the poor. I still have to look after Rosa, and then the young man may have his way, and I want to die too. What am I doing here in this endless winter! My horse is dead, and there is no one in the village who'll lend me his. I have to drag my team out of the pig sty. If they hadn't happened to be horses, I'd have had to travel with pigs. That's the way it is. And I nod to the family. They know nothing about it, and if they did know, they wouldn't believe it. Incidentally, it's easy to write prescriptions, but difficult to come to an understanding with people. Now, at this point my visit might have come to an end—they have once more called for my help unnecessarily. I'm used to that. With the help of my night bell the entire region torments me, but that this time I had to sacrifice Rosa as well, this beautiful girl, who lives in my house all year long and whom I scarcely notice—this sacrifice is too great, and I must somehow in my own head subtly rationalize it away for the moment, in order not to let loose at this family who cannot, even with their best will, give me Rosa back again. But as I am closing up my handbag and calling for my fur coat, the family is standing together, the father sniffing the glass of rum in his hand, the mother, probably disappointed in me—what more do these people expect?—tearfully biting her lips, and the sister flapping a very bloody hand towel, I am somehow ready, in the circumstances, to concede that the young man is perhaps nonetheless sick. I go to him. He smiles up at me, as if I was bringing him the most nourishing kind of soup—ah, now both horses are whinnying, the noise is probably supposed to come from higher regions in order to illuminate my examination—and now I find out that, yes indeed, the young man is ill. On his right side, in the region of the hip, a wound the size of the palm of one's hand has opened up. Rose colored, in many different shadings, dark in the depths, brighter on the edges, delicately grained, with uneven patches of blood, open to the light like a mine. That's what it looks like from a distance. Close up a complication is apparent. Who can look at that without whistling softly? Worms, as thick and long as my little finger, themselves rose colored and also spattered with blood, are wriggling their white bodies with many limbs from their stronghold in the inner of the wound toward the light. Poor young man, there's no helping you. I have found out your great wound. You are dying from this flower on your side. The family is happy; they see me doing something. The sister says that to the mother, the mother tells the father, the father tells a few guests who are coming in on tiptoe through the moonlight of the open door, balancing themselves with outstretched arms. "Will you save me?" whispers the young man, sobbing, quite blinded by the life inside his wound. That's how people are in my region. Always demanding the impossible from the doctor. They have lost the old faith. The priest sits at home and tears his religious robes to pieces, one after the other. But the doctor is supposed to achieve everything with his delicate surgeon's hand. Well, it's what they like to think. I have not offered myself. If they use me for sacred purposes, I let that happen to me as well. What more do I want, an old country doctor, robbed of my servant girl! And they come, the families and the village elders, and take my clothes off. A choir of school children with the teacher at the head stands in front of the house and sings an extremely simple melody with the words:

> Take his clothes off, then he'll heal,
> and if he doesn't cure, then kill him.
> It's only a doctor; it's only a doctor.

story ends next p.

Then I am stripped of my clothes and, with my fingers in my beard and my head tilted to one side, I look at the people quietly. I am completely calm and clear about everything and stay that way, too, although it is not helping me at all, for they are now taking me by the head and feet and dragging me into bed. They lay me against the wall on the side of wound. Then they all go out of the room. The door is shut. The singing stops. Clouds move in front of the moon. The bedclothes lie warmly around me. In the open space of the windows the horses' heads sway like shadows. "Do you know," I hear someone saying in my ear, "my confidence in you is very small. You were shaken out from somewhere. You don't come on your own feet. Instead of helping, you give me less room on my deathbed. The best thing would be if I scratch your eyes out."

"Right," I say, "it's a disgrace. But now I'm a doctor. What am I supposed to do? Believe me, things are not easy for me either."

"Should I be satisfied with this excuse? Alas, I'll probably have to be. I always have to make do. I came into the world with a beautiful wound; that was all I was furnished with."

"Young friend," I say, "your mistake is that you have no perspective. I've already been in all the sick rooms, far and wide, and I tell you your wound is not so bad. Made in a tight corner with two blows from an axe. Many people offer their side and hardly hear the axe in the forest, to say nothing of the fact that it's coming closer to them."

"Is that really so, or are you deceiving me in my fever?"

"It is truly so. Take the word of honor of a medical doctor." He took my word and grew still. But now it was time to think about my escape. The horses were still standing loyally in place. Clothes, fur coat, and bag were quickly snatched up. I didn't want to delay by getting dressed; if the horses rushed as they had on the journey out, I should, in fact, be springing out of that bed into my own, as it were. One horse obediently pulled back from the window. I threw the bundle into the carriage. The fur coat flew too far and was caught on a hook by only one arm. Good enough. I swung myself up onto the horse. The reins dragging loosely, one horse barely harnessed to the other, the carriage swaying behind, last of all the fur coat in the snow. "Giddy up," I said, but there was no giddying up about it. We dragged through the snowy desert like old men; for a long time the fresh but inaccurate singing of the children resounded behind us:

> Enjoy yourselves, you patients.
> The doctor's laid in bed with you.

I'll never come home at this rate. My flourishing practice is lost. A successor is robbing me, but to no avail, for he cannot replace me. In my house the disgusting groom is wreaking havoc. Rosa is his victim. I will not think it through. Naked, abandoned to the frost of this unhappy age, with an earthly carriage and unearthly horses, I drive around by myself, an old man. My fur coat hangs behind the wagon, but I cannot reach it, and no one from the nimble rabble of patients lifts a finger. Betrayed! Betrayed! Once one responds to a false alarm on the night bell, there's no making it good again—not ever.

A REPORT FOR AN ACADEMY

Esteemed Gentlemen of the Academy!

You show me the honor of calling upon me to submit a report to the Academy concerning my previous life as an ape.

In this sense, unfortunately, I cannot comply with your request. Almost five years separate me from my existence as an ape, a short time perhaps when measured by the calendar, but endlessly long to gallop through, as I have done, at times accompanied by splendid men, advice, applause, and orchestral music, but basically alone, since all those accompanying me held themselves back a long way from the barrier, in order to preserve the image. This achievement would have been impossible if I had stubbornly wished to hold onto my origin, onto the memories of my youth.

Giving up that obstinacy[1] was, in fact, the highest command that I gave myself. I, a free ape, submitted myself to this yoke.[2] In so doing, however, my memories for their part constantly closed themselves off against me. If people had wanted it, my journey back at first would have been possible through the entire gateway which heaven builds over the earth, but as my development was whipped onward, the gate simultaneously grew lower and narrower all the time. I felt myself more comfortable and more enclosed in the world of human beings. The storm which blew

---

[1] Stubbornness.

[2] In this context: mark or symbol of subjection.

me out of my past eased off. Today it is only a gentle breeze which cools my heels. And the distant hole through which it comes and through which I once came has become so small that, even if I had sufficient power and will to run back there, I would have to scrape the fur off my body in order to get through. Speaking frankly, as much as I like choosing metaphors for these things— speaking frankly: your experience as apes, gentlemen—to the extent that you have something of that sort behind you—cannot be more distant from you than mine is from me. But it tickles at the heels of everyone who walks here on earth, the small chimpanzee as well as the great Achilles.[3]

In the narrowest sense, however, I can perhaps answer your question, nonetheless, and indeed I do so with great pleasure.

The first thing I learned was to give a handshake. The handshake displays candor.[4] Today, when I stand at the highpoint of my career, may I add to that first handshake also my candid words. For the Academy it will not provide anything essentially new and will fall far short of what people have asked of me and what with the best will I cannot speak about—but nonetheless it should demonstrate the line by which someone who was an ape was forced into the world of men and which he has continued there. Yet I would certainly not permit myself to say even the trivial things which follow if I were not completely sure of myself and if my position on all the great music hall stages of the civilized world had not established itself unassailably.

I come from the Gold Coast.[5] For an account of how I was captured I rely on the reports of strangers. A hunting expedition from the firm of Hagenback—incidentally, since then I have already emptied a number of bottles of good red wine with the leader of that expedition—lay hidden in the bushes by the shore when I ran down in the evening in the middle of a band of apes

---

[3] The greatest Greek warrior in the Trojan War and hero of the Homer's *Iliad*.

[4] The quality of being frank, open, and sincere.

[5] Gold Coast is a coastal city and a region in the state of Queensland, Australia.

for a drink. Someone fired a shot. I was the only one struck. I received two hits.

One was in the cheek—that was superficial. But it left behind a large hairless red scar which earned me the name Red Peter—a revolting name, completely inappropriate, presumably something invented by an ape, as if the only difference between me and the recently deceased trained ape Peter, who was well known here and there, was the red patch on my cheek. But this is only by the way.

The second shot hit me below the hip. It was serious. It's the reason that today I still limp a little. Recently I read in an article by one of the ten thousand gossipers who vent their opinions about me in the newspapers that my ape nature is not yet entirely repressed. The proof is that when visitors come I take pleasure in pulling off my trousers to show the entry wound caused by this shot. That fellow should have each finger of his writing hand shot off one by one. So far as I am concerned, I may pull my trousers down in front of anyone I like. People will not find there anything other than well cared for fur and the scar from—let us select here a precise word for a precise purpose, something that will not be misunderstood—the scar from a wicked shot. Everything is perfectly open; there is nothing to hide. When it comes to a question of the truth, every great mind discards the most subtle refinements of manners. However, if that writer were to pull down his trousers when he gets a visitor, that would certainly produce a different sight, and I'll take it as a sign of reason that he does not do that. But then he should not bother me with his delicate sensibilities.

After those shots I woke up—and here my own memory gradually begins—in a cage between decks on the Hagenbeck steamship. It was no four-sided cage with bars, but only three walls fixed to a crate, so that the crate constituted the fourth wall. The whole thing was too low to stand upright and too narrow for sitting down. So I crouched with bent knees, which shook all the time, and since at first I probably did not wish to see anyone and to remain constantly in the darkness, I turned toward the crate,

story ends p. 146

while the bars of the cage cut into the flesh on my back. People consider such confinement of wild animals beneficial in the very first period of time, and today I cannot deny, on the basis of my own experience, that in a human sense that is, in fact, the case.

But at that time I didn't think about it. For the first time in my life I was without a way out—at least there was no direct way out. Right in front of me was the crate, its boards fitted closely together. Well, there was a hole running right through the boards. When I first discovered it, I welcomed it with a blissfully happy howl of ignorance. But this hole was not nearly big enough to stick my tail through, and all the power of an ape could not make it any bigger.

According to what I was told later, I am supposed to have made remarkably little noise. From that people concluded that either I must soon die or, if I succeeded in surviving the first critical period, I would be very capable of being trained. I survived this period. Muffled sobbing, painfully searching out fleas, wearily licking a coconut, banging my skull against the wall of the crate, sticking out my tongue when anyone came near—these were the first occupations in my new life. In all of them, however, there was only one feeling: no way out. Nowadays, of course, I can portray those ape-like feelings only with human words and, as a result, I misrepresent them. But even if I can no longer attain the old truth of the ape, at least it lies in the direction I have described—of that there is no doubt.

Up until then I had had so many ways out, and now I no longer had one. I was tied down. If they had nailed me down, my freedom to move would not have been any less. And why? If you scratch raw the flesh between your toes, you won't find the reason. If you press your back against the bars of the cage until it almost slices you in two, you won't find the answer. I had no way out, but I had to come up with one for myself. For without that I could not live. Always in front of that crate wall—I would inevitably have died a miserable death. But according to Hagenbeck, apes belong at the crate wall—well, that meant I had to cease being an ape. A clear and beautiful train of thought, which I must have planned somehow with my belly, since apes think with their bellies.

I'm worried that people do not understand precisely what I mean by a way out. I use the word in its most common and fullest sense. I am deliberately not saying freedom. I do not mean this great feeling of freedom on all sides. As an ape, I perhaps recognized it, and I have met human beings who yearn for it. But as far as I am concerned, I did not demand freedom either then or today. Incidentally, among human beings people all too often are deceived by freedom. And since freedom is reckoned among the most sublime feelings, the corresponding disappointment is also among the most sublime. In the variety shows, before my entrance, I have often watched a pair of artists busy on trapezes high up in the roof. They swung themselves, they rocked back and forth, they jumped, they hung in each other's arms, one held the other by clenching the hair with his teeth. 'That, too, is human freedom,' I thought, 'self-controlled movement.' What a mockery of sacred nature! At such a sight, no structure would stand up to the laughter of the apes.

No, I didn't want freedom. Only a way out—to the right or left or anywhere at all. I made no other demands, even if the way out should be only an illusion. The demand was small; the disappointment would not be any greater—to move on further, to move on further! Only not to stand still with arms raised, pressed against a crate wall.

Today I see clearly that without the greatest inner calm I would never have been able to get out. And in fact I probably owe everything that I have become to the calmness which came over me after the first days there on the ship. And, in turn, I owe that calmness to the people on the ship.

They are good people, in spite of everything. Today I still enjoy remembering the clang of their heavy steps, which used to echo then in my half sleep. They had the habit of tackling every-thing extremely slowly. If one of them wanted to rub his eyes, he raised his hand as if it were a hanging weight. Their jokes were gross but hearty. Their laughter was always mixed with a rasp

story ends p. 146

which sounded dangerous but meant nothing. They always had something in their mouths to spit out, and they didn't care where they spat. They always complained that my fleas sprung over onto them, but they were never seriously angry at me because of it. They even knew that fleas liked being in my fur and that fleas are jumpers. They learned to live with that. When they had no duties, sometimes a few of them sat down in a semi-circle around me. They didn't speak much, but only made noises to each other and smoked their pipes, stretched out on the crates. They slapped their knees as soon as I made the slightest movement, and from time to time one of them would pick up a stick and tickle me where I liked it. If I were invited today to make a journey on that ship, I'd certainly decline the invitation, but it's equally certain that the memories I could dwell on of the time there between the decks would not be totally hateful.

The calmness which I acquired in this circle of people prevented me above all from any attempt to escape. Looking at it nowadays, it seems to me as if I had at least sensed that I had to find a way out if I wanted to live, but that this way out could not be reached by escaping. I no longer know if escape was possible, but I think it was: for an ape it should always be possible to flee. With my present teeth I have to be careful even with the ordinary task of cracking a nut, but then I must have been able, over time, to succeed in chewing through the lock on the door. I didn't do that. What would I have achieved by doing that? No sooner would I have stuck my head out, than they would have captured me again and locked me up in an even worse cage. Or I could have taken refuge unnoticed among the other animals—say, the boa constrictors opposite me—and breathed my last in their embraces. Or I could have managed to steal way up to the deck and jumped overboard. Then I'd have tossed back and forth for a while on the ocean and drowned. Acts of despair. I did not think things through in such a human way, but under the influence of my surroundings conducted myself as if I had worked things out.

I did not work things out, but I observed well in complete tranquility. I saw these men going back and forth, always the same faces, the same movements. Often it seemed to me as if there was only one man. So the man or these men went undisturbed. A lofty purpose dawned on me. No one promised me that if I could become like them the cage would be removed. Such promises, apparently impossible to fulfill, were not made. But if one makes the fulfillment good, then later the promises appear precisely there where one had looked for them earlier without success. Now, these men in themselves were nothing which attracted me very much. If I had been a follower of that freedom I just mentioned, I would certainly have preferred the ocean to the way out displayed in the dull gaze of these men. But in any case, I observed them for a long time before I even thought about such things—in fact, the accumulated observations first pushed me in the proper direction.

It was so easy to imitate these people. I could already spit on the first day. We used to spit in each other's faces. The only difference was that I licked my face clean afterward. They did not. Soon I was smoking a pipe, like an old man, and if I then pressed my thumb down into the bowl of the pipe, the entire area between decks cheered. Still, for a long time I did not understand the difference between an empty and a full pipe.

I had the greatest difficulty with the bottle of alcohol. The smell was torture to me. I forced myself with all my power, but weeks went by before I could overcome my reaction. Curiously enough, the people took this inner struggle more seriously than anything else about me. In my memories I don't distinguish the people, but there was one who always came back, alone or with comrades, day and night, at different times. He'd stand with a bottle in front of me and give me instructions. He did not understand me. He wanted to solve the riddle of my being. He used to uncork the bottle slowly and then look at me, in order to test if I had understood. I confess that I always looked at him with wildly over-eager attentiveness. No human teacher has ever found in the entire world such a student of human beings.

After he'd uncorked the bottle, he'd raise it to his mouth. I'd gaze at him, right at his throat. He would nod, pleased with

story ends p. 146

me, and set the bottle to his lips. Delighted with my gradual understanding, I'd squeal and scratch myself all over, wherever it was convenient. He was happy. He'd set the bottle to his mouth and take a swallow. Impatient and desperate to emulate him, I would defecate over myself in my cage—and that again gave him great satisfaction. Then, holding the bottle at arm's length and bringing it up again with a swing, he'd drink it down with one gulp, exaggerating his backward bending as a way of instructing me. Exhausted with so much great effort, I could no longer follow and hung weakly onto the bars, while he ended the theoretical lesson by rubbing his belly and grinning.

Now the practical exercises first began. Was I not already too tired out by the theoretical part? Yes, indeed, far too weary. That's part of my fate. Nonetheless, I'd grab the proffered bottle as well as I could and uncork it trembling. Once I'd managed to do that, new forces gradually take over. I lift the bottle—with hardly any difference between me and the original—put it to my lips—and throw it away in disgust, in disgust, although it is empty and filled only with the smell, throw it with disgust onto the floor. To the sorrow of my teacher, to my own greater sorrow. And I still do not console him or myself when, after throwing away the bottle, I do not forget to give my belly a splendid rub and to grin as I do so.

All too often, the lesson went that way. And to my teacher's credit, he was not angry with me. Well, sometimes he held his burning pipe against my fur in some place or other which I could reach only with difficulty, until it began to burn. But then he would put it out himself with his huge good hand. He wasn't angry with me. He realized that we were fighting on the same side against ape nature and that I had the more difficult part.

What a victory it was for him and for me, however, when one evening in front of a large circle of onlookers—perhaps it was a celebration, a gramophone[6] was playing, and officer was wandering around among the people—when on this evening,

---

[6] An old-fashioned record player.

at a moment when no one was watching, I grabbed a bottle of alcohol which had been inadvertently left standing in front of my cage, uncorked it just as I had been taught, amid the rising attention of the group, set it against my mouth and, without hesitating, with my mouth making no grimace, like an expert drinker, with my eyes rolling around, splashing the liquid in my throat, I really and truly drank the bottle empty, and then threw it away, no longer in despair, but like an artist. Well, I did forget to scratch my belly. But instead of that, because I couldn't do anything else, because I had to, because my senses were roaring, I cried out a short and good 'Hello!' breaking out into human sounds. And with this cry I sprang into the community of human beings, and I felt its echo—'Just listen. He's talking!'—like a kiss on my entire sweat-soaked body.

I'll say it again: imitating human beings was not something which pleased me. I imitated them because I was looking for a way out, for no other reason. And even in that victory little was achieved. My voice immediately failed me again. It first came back months later. My distaste for the bottle of alcohol became even stronger. But at least my direction was given to me once and for all.

When I was handed over in Hamburg to my first trainer, I soon realized the two possibilities open to me: the Zoological Garden or the Music Hall. I did not hesitate. I said to myself: use all your energy to get into the Music Hall. That is the way out. The Zoological Garden is only a new barred cage. If you go there, you're lost.

And I learned, gentlemen. Alas, one learns when one has to. One learns when one wants a way out. One learns ruthlessly. One supervises oneself with a whip and tears oneself apart at the slightest resistance. My ape nature ran off, head over heels, out of me, so that in the process my first teacher himself almost became an ape and soon had to give up training and be carried off to a mental hospital. Fortunately he was soon discharged again.

But I went through many teachers—indeed, even several teachers at once. As I became more confident of my abilities

story ends next p.

and the general public followed my progress and my future began to brighten, I took on teachers myself, let them sit down in five interconnected rooms, and studied with them all simultaneously, by constantly leaping from one room into another.

And such progress! The penetrating effects of the rays of knowledge from all sides on my awaking brain! I don't deny the fact—I was delighted with it. But I also confess that I did not overestimate it, not even then, even less today. With an effort which up to this point has never been repeated on earth, I have attained the average education of a European. That would perhaps not amount to much, but it is something insofar as it helped me out of the cage and created this special way out for me—the way out of human beings. There is an excellent German expression: to beat one's way through the bushes. That I have done. I have beaten my way through the bushes. I had no other way, always assuming that freedom was not a choice.

If I review my development and its goal up to this point, I do not complain. I am even satisfied. With my hands in my trouser pockets, the bottle of wine on the table, I half lie and half sit in my rocking chair and gaze out the window. If I have a visitor, I welcome him as is appropriate. My impresario sits in the parlor. If I ring, he comes and listens to what I have to say. In the evening I almost always have a performance, and my success could hardly rise any higher. When I come home late from banquets, from scientific societies, or from social gatherings in someone's home, a small half-trained female chimpanzee is waiting for me, and I take my pleasure with her the way apes do. During the day I don't want to see her. For she has in her gaze the madness of a bewildered trained animal. I'm the only one who recognizes that, and I cannot bear it.

On the whole, at any rate, I have achieved what I wished to achieve. You shouldn't say it wasn't worth the effort. In any case, I don't want any man's judgment. I only want to expand knowledge. I simply report. Even to you, esteemed gentlemen of the Academy, I have only made a report.

Franz Kafka

*The insect itself is
not to be drawn.
It is not even to be
seen from a distance.

— Franz Kafka